MURDER IS GRIM

MURDER IS GRIM

If Kate Archer had known just what the invitation entailed, she most certainly would not have succumbed to the pleading of June Gladstone to spend a month's vacation at her father's luxurious farm.

Kate had met June at school, and, although four years her senior, had gone out of her way to befriend the forlorn, unattractive, almost ugly girl in her early teens.

Now, five years later, the invitation had appeared out of the blue, and Kate found herself a guest in a strange, isolated household of *very* bohemian ways, with a menacing undercurrent that made Kate very uneasy.

Suddenly, things began to happen with astonishing rapidity. Clotilde, June's beautiful stepsister was kidnapped in very gruesome circumstances, and Kate had to play a nerve-racking part in delivering the ransom money.

But two murders occurred before peace was finally restored in the Gladstone household, and the warped, twisted mind of a murderer was revealed.

MURDER IS GRIM

by

SAMUEL ROGERS

WILDSIDE PRESS

First published in Great Britain in 1955
This book was first published in the U.S.A. under the title "You'll be Sorry"

Chapter One

KATE ARCHER studied the strange note she had just been reading, wrinkled her forehead, and stooped to rescue the envelope from the basket beside her desk. She realized now that the stiff handwriting was actually printing, though this was not so obvious in black as it was in the red crayon of the enclosed message:

DON'T GO TO MR. GLADSTONE'S. YOU'LL BE SORRY IF YOU DO.

What she felt, after her first moment of sheer surprise, was more than anything annoyance at the unreasonableness of her correspondent: here she was to be called for within the next hour; even if she wanted to, there would be no time now to change her plans. Then the next instant she was ashamed at having considered any change. 'If he thinks a childish trick like this will have the slightest effect on what I do,' she muttered to herself, 'he's very much mistaken.'

But who was 'He'? Even an anonymous letter must be written by someone with a name. Who would not want her to go to Mr. Gladstone's? Of course Mother was disappointed; she had hoped that Kate would come East now, to spend the whole summer at Matunuck, instead of staying out here for another month, to visit in the Middle West; but it was absurd to think of Mother's writing this; Mother would never try to scare her, even in fun.

She caught herself up sharply and glanced about the quiet room. Whatever she felt it was not fear; she would not give 'Him' that satisfaction! The envelope, she now noticed, was postmarked *Woodside*, and was dated June 14th; to-day was Thursday, the 15th; it had been mailed here in town yesterday afternoon.

Could it be one of the young men who had asked her to marry him during this last year at the university? She thought of her fellow-students, of her lab instructors. Rejected suitors, she had discovered were apt to feel that in a way she had deceived them – not by any definite action but just by the fact of her own nature: each one had told her that at first she had seemed so 'sweet', so gentle; they could not understand her growing bored, or even impatient, at their persistence. She never pretended – certainly she never tried – to be 'sweet'. If they thought she was, it was largely because of her appearance: her dark golden hair, her blue eyes, her fine skin and softly 'classic' features; and for some reason boys seemed to think that that combination went with sweetness of nature; but it was also because she did hate to make people unhappy, because she couldn't help being kind and pleasant to them at first – and then suddenly they would be in love with her, and she had to make them understand that she was not in love with them. But surely none of these boys would stoop to such a petty revenge, even if in some way they had learned of her visit.

Kate continued to frown. She would have hated to think that someone she knew, someone she liked, had written this letter; and yet it would have been comforting to be able to place it, to lift it out of the realm of the mysterious. She looked once more around the small room, so intensely silent, where she had studied for so many hours during the past winter. All her things that had not been sent off earlier were now packed in the two big suitcases standing side by side near the door. The room looked unnaturally neat and stripped. There was nothing on the bureau, nothing on the table; the framed photographs, the brilliant

van Gogh print, had gone from the walls. Afternoon sunlight streaming across the threadbare blue carpet seemed
to touch it with strangeness, as if it were the carpet in
some huge impersonal second-hand store: this silent place
had withdrawn into itself; it was waiting for her to get out.

She glanced at her watch. It was quarter to three and
Mr. Gladstone had written that she would be called for at
three; but she walked over to the window and looked
down through the box-elder boughs. Perhaps the car
might be early. The short street was empty except for some
boys playing ball in front of the apartment house at the
corner. Kate wondered from which direction the car
would appear, what kind of car it would be. Would Mr.
Gladstone be driving it himself? And what would Mr.
Gladstone be like?

DON'T GO TO MR. GLADSTONE'S.

For an instant she could see a pale fixed face that stared
straight ahead at the road from under its hatbrim, that
would not look at her until suddenly in a lonely place the
car stopped, the driver raised his hands to the back of his
head and she could see that his face was a mask. He was
taking it off, he was going to stare at her now, but he had
no eyes, no features. She could not bear to look.

YOU'LL BE SORRY IF YOU DO.

This was absurd, she thought angrily. How pleased the
writer of the letter would be! But she could form so little
idea of her month at Mr. Gladstone's that it was impossible to imagine its beginning, to picture a car turning one
of these corners, to the left or to the right, and stopping
there below in front of the house; just as sometimes when
you wait at the telephone for a long-distance call, you

can't believe that the voice you are expecting will actually break that silence.

Might the warning have been sent by anyone in the Gladstone household? But who could it be, when June, the only one she knew, was' so' terribly eager for her to come? She took June's letter, the first she had received from her in more than two years, out of her purse, and read it slowly once again:

Dear Katey,

It's crazy that you've been at Woodside for a whole year and I live only twenty miles away and we haven't seen each other. You bad girl, why didn't you write me you were there? I just found out by chance from a girl at school who says she knows your brother. Of course I've been away at school except for holidays so we wouldn't have had much chance to get together. But now I'm home for the summer and I want you to come and visit me for at least a month. Father says why should someone that's really grown up and finishing college want to bury herself out here with a schoolgirl like me, but he doesn't know about you and me, does he? I guess no one could understand that.

I bet all sorts of things have been happening to you since the old days at Miss Barstow's. Nothing at all has happened to me, at least nothing nice, just two other schools, after Miss Barstow's, and I hated them both just as much. I really hated them more because you weren't there, and I never found anyone else to be really nice to me the way you were. There's something wrong with me, Katey. You used to say there wasn't but I know there is, because I try to be nice to people but nobody likes me. It may be just because I'm so damn ugly and clumsy. I can hear you scolding me now for that 'damn'. It just slipped out. If you come I give you

permission to scold me as much as you like, and I
promise not to get mad the way I used to.

Honestly, Katey, I can't tell you how much I want
you to come. I'll be watching the mail every day for
your answer, so be quick, won't you? I can't bear having
to wait for things I want.

With loads of love,

Your bad 'little* June'

* Only I'm not little any more. I wish I was.

Kate had replied affectionately but had said that she
could not come. She had not seen June Gladstone in four
years, and remembered her as a dumpy girl whom everyone ignored and who had seemed to go her way in rather
morose indifference until the afternoon when Kate discovered her lying on the grass behind the summerhouse,
her body shaken with sobs. It was because she was lonely,
June explained, after Kate had coaxed her to talk, because
everyone despised her. Kate had put her arm around her,
had quieted her at last, and got permission from Miss
Spencer to take her to Johnson's for a chocolate sundae.

After that, for the rest of the year, June had dogged her
footsteps to an almost embarrassing extent, never talking
much, never making any demands, but glaring like some
fierce dark little animal at any girl to whom Kate paid
much attention. Just before the end of the spring term she
had been mysteriously expelled, and when Kate, who had
come to feel rather responsible for her, had questioned the
headmistress, Miss Barstow had explained that some 'bad
books' had been found in her bureau drawer. 'To do June
justice,' she had gone on, 'her family background, from
what I can gather, isn't at all what it should be. I feel
very sorry for her. I'm quite sure her parents are more to
blame than she is, but there was nothing else to do, for
the sake of the school.'

Kate had smiled to herself, with some indignation, at the thought of poor little June's corrupting her so much more sophisticated schoolmates. She had thought at the time, and she still suspected, that the books, whatever they were, had been planted in June's drawer by one of the girls who disliked her, who were jealous of the way that Kate had taken her under her wing; but June had already gone, there would be no way of proving such a plot; and in the letters Kate and she had exchanged for the next two years, letters which had grown more and more scarce, neither one had ever alluded to the affair.

Kate had refused this summer's invitation chiefly because she was so eager to get home, to see Mother, to bask in the sun on the long white beach; but she had felt a little guilty and more than a little curious. June had never spoken a word to her of any sort about her family. During Kate's year in Woodside she had heard rumours of the Gladstone estate out by the river, and the 'things that went on' there. A week after June's letter, she had received one from Mr. Gladstone himself, urging her to come; she had accepted then, though without committing herself as to how long she would stay, because she knew that if she refused, her conscience would bother her all summer.

She folded June's letter now, put it back in her purse, and took out Mr. Gladstone's, frowning a little as she tried to decipher once more the bold careless-looking script.

Dear Miss Archer,

God knows I detest people who interfere with other people's business, and I think my record is pretty clear on that score. My excuse for writing you now is that you can tear this up, if you like, and not give it another thought. I'd be the first to sympathize with you.

The fact is, June is so desperately disappointed that

you won't visit us that I said I'd see what I could do.
Let me give you an idea of the general set-up. We live
in what might be described as the deep country, out by
the river. There is no suitable person approaching June's
age in the neighbourhood, and she is terribly lonely and
restless. I should mention, perhaps, if she hasn't, that she
has an older sister, about your age. If June were different and if Clotilde were different, that might fix
things up – but you know what families are. Or perhaps
you don't. If not, you'll learn when you have one of
your own.

I can quite understand that a month's tête-à-tête with
a girl like June may not seem too exciting for a girl four
years (so June tells me) older than she. Let me reassure
you that in the first place it will not be a tête-à-tête.
We're quite a little group out here, and if we're too old
to suit a girl of sixteen, I'm sure that some of us won't
seem too senile for a young woman of twenty.

But if what June says about you is true, the induce-
ments to dangle before you are not the things you may
receive but the things you may be able to give. You can
give June, I believe, a period of really intense happiness,
which she will appreciate all the more because that is
something, I'm afraid, that on the whole she hasn't
known very much of. One of my reasons for urging you
is no doubt that, as a father, I haven't been a startling
success. Naturally the easiest way to quiet my paternal
conscience is to find a friend of hers who might to some
extent compensate for my shortcomings. Since you have
known June, you don't have to be told that when she
wants something she wants it very much indeed, and I
can truthfully say I've never known her to want anything so much as to have you visit her.

Sincerely (and hopefully) yours,

Norman Gladstone

It was a queer letter. She did not like it very well, but certainly Mr. Gladstone was eager for her to come. It would be wholly unreasonable to send her such a letter as this, and then follow it up with an anonymous warning to keep away.

A knock at the door startled her so that she dropped her letter on the rug. After she had picked it up, she glanced once more out of the window. An empty car was parked in front of the house, a magnificent grass-green convertible than which nothing could be less sinister. 'I'm afraid I'm not meant to live alone', she thought.

She walked quickly to the door, opened it, and smiled at the man who stood in the doorway. He had a real face, there was no doubt of that; he was medium-sized, about forty, with blunt features, thin hair, and a neat brown moustache. As a matter of fact, everything about him looked exceptionally neat – his dark blue suit, his black necktie, the very way he stood, easy and erect and somehow shipshape. His brown eyes looked softly and brightly into hers.

'Is this Miss Archer?' he asked, and his voice seemed to fit his appearance – gentle, firm and efficient.

'Yes, it is,' she said, 'and I suppose you're Mr. Gladstone.'

He smiled. 'Far from it', he exclaimed. 'I'm just the chauffeur, the gardener, the man of all work. My name is Felix Brownell.'

Kate noticed now that his dark suit, his tie, had the suggestion of a uniform or livery. She felt embarrassed. 'Oh, I'm so sorry,' she said, 'Mr. Brownell.'

'Don't apologize', he told her. 'It's a compliment. As a matter of fact, I've been with the family so long I almost feel as if I was part of it. And by the way, of course you must call me Felix.'

'Oh, well – yes, I will', Kate said, still rather self-conscious. She suspected that for some time at least she would call him only 'you'.

'I assume these are your bags, miss?' He stepped into the room and picked them up easily. She was sure that he had added the 'miss' simply to put her at her ease.

'I'm afraid they're very heavy.'

'You should feel Mr. Gladstone's, or for that matter, Miss Clotilde's. I'll be taking them down. If you have anyone to say good-bye to —'

'No, there's no one', she said. She took a last glance at the room, shut the door quickly, as if she were shutting her nervousness inside, and followed him down the stairs.

It gave her a luxurious feeling to step into the big shiny car. As she settled back on the dark green leather cushions it seemed to her that she could not imagine a more comfortable seat.

'If you'd prefer to sit in the back,' Felix said, 'I can put up the top, but otherwise, I'm afraid, it would be too windy.'

'I'd much rather sit here', she said. 'That is, if you don't mind.'

'Personally, I always prefer company when I'm driving', he said in a courtly tone. 'Which reminds me: June said be sure and tell you she'd have driven in with me, except that I left this morning right after breakfast. I've been doing the week's marketing, and selling stuff from the farm.'

He started the car so smoothly and the motor was so silent that Kate was surprised to see that they were already moving. In ten minutes they were out of town, had skirted the end of the lake, and were driving westward through the rolling fields, the patches of oak forest, that surrounded Woodside. It was a lovely afternoon, with a few clouds softly brushing the treetops and the telephone wires. The air smelled of white clover and as the breeze touched her

face she felt that it had still kept something of the remote-
ness of the farthest hills.

She was trying to think up a friendly remark to make to
Felix, when he spoke himself.

'You know,' he said, with his eyes fixed on the road, 'I'm
glad you're going to be visiting us at Valley Farms. June
needs someone, some nice pleasant young lady like you,
to keep her company. I hope that doesn't sound impertinent.'

'Not at all', Kate said. 'I'm glad you think I'll be of
some use. Of course June does have a sister, doesn't
she?'

For a moment he merely pursed his lips. 'Clotilde is
very attractive', he said at last, and Kate noticed that he
had dropped the 'Miss' before her name. 'She's the beauty
of the family, you know. But between ourselves, I don't
think she's much of a help to June. You'll see soon enough.
Of course they are only half-sisters. You probably know
all about that.'

'No, I didn't know it', Kate said. 'I never even knew
June had a sister until I got Mr. Gladstone's letter. And
who else is at the farm? I don't know anything about the
family really. I haven't even met Mr. Gladstone.'

'Well, there's Mrs. Gladstone, June's mother – everyone
calls her Mavis, even the girls. And just now there's Mr.
Green; he's Clotilde's fiancé. They're going to be married
in a few weeks, I guess. I shouldn't be surprised if they ran
off any time. And there's Jo, or I should say Mr. Martinez.
He's Spanish.'

'But who is he?' she asked. 'What does he do?'

'He's a violinist. They say he's very good.'

'But I mean is he a relation? Is he connected with the
family?'

Felix hesitated again and again pursed his lips; Kate
could see that he disapproved of Jo.

'No – he's not a relation', he said slowly. 'You might say he's just a kind of – special friend.'

For a long time neither spoke. It seemed as if the thought of Jo had dried up Felix's sociability; and Kate found that the breeze as it lapped around the side of the windshield, the monotony of woodland and meadow, were lulling her into a pleasant drowsiness. She did notice, however, that the hills were growing higher, the farmhouses somewhat less frequent. Now and then a spur of rock jutted out from the end of a wooded ridge like the prow of a gigantic ship. She noticed, too, how Felix always kept the car at exactly thirty-five miles, whether they were going up hill or down; she could imagine that she was floating through the sky, a summer sky endlessly blue and soft, floating above a region of green silent waves.

Then, without warning, the car stopped.

In a flash she recalled her imaginings in her room a little while ago, and glanced at Felix. But Felix was leaning out of the car and talking to a thickset middle-aged man, with sharp features and bright bird-like eyes, who was sitting on a bank, with a bicycle leaning against the turf beside him. They were near the top of the highest hill so far, and he had evidently stopped to rest.

'Well, Professor,' Felix asked, 'can I give you a lift? You look just about all in. Men our age oughtn't to attempt long bicycle rides in summer – especially with these hills.'

Kate smiled at Felix's tact: this stranger must be ten years older than he.

'It's all very well for you to talk,' the man replied in a precise voice, 'with your boss getting gas for two cars, and then wangling a C card out of his ration board. I should think he'd be ashamed of himself.'

Felix shrugged his shoulders and his flickering smile became for a moment almost a grin. 'Well, there are no trains around here; there are no buses. And we have to get our produce to market. When I drove to town to-day the trunk was full of fresh vegetables. Mostly lettuce.'

The man with the bicycle stood up and slowly shook one leg, then the other. 'Well, if he can get away with it, who am I to object? There are worse things than that the matter with the Roosevelt régime. But as far as buses and trains go, they don't come any nearer me than they do you. And I'm farther from the main road.'

'Perhaps they don't think your work out here is essential to the war effort', Felix suggested. Then turning to Kate, he explained: 'Professor Hatfield spends his vacations by the river looking for birds.'

'Wherever the gas comes from, I'd gladly accept a lift', Professor Hatfield went on. 'But what about the bicycle?'

'We can fix that in behind', Felix said; and the next moment he was in the road and, rather to Kate's alarm, because the car looked so spotless, he was lifting the bicycle into the back seat. In a couple of minutes he had arranged it so that it rested firmly propped, without a scratch to the paint or the rich green leather.

'But I haven't introduced you, have I?' he went on to Kate. 'You must think I'm very rude. Professor, I take pleasure in presenting you to Miss Katherine Archer. Since she goes to the university, she's probably heard of you. She's coming out to visit June, and I hope she won't think me fresh if I say I can't imagine a more charming visitor.'

Kate recalled Professor Hatfield's name, and thought now that she remembered having seen him about the campus. His eyes were fixed intently upon her; he cocked his head so as to get a clearer view, and for that moment he reminded her of a smooth, alert, but rather dusty parrot.

'June is very lucky,' he said, 'to have such a friend. I

hope I won't crowd you, Miss Archer. At any rate I'm several pounds thinner than when I started out after 'unch.'

: Kate was thoroughly enjoying herself; she was growing quite fond of Felix, now that he no longer surprised her, and thought she would like this friendly sharp-eyed gentleman.

'Are you an ornithologist?' she asked as the car slipped smoothly over the crest of the hill. 'I always thought you were in the chemistry department.'

'I earn my living teaching chemistry,' he said, 'and just now I'm doing research for our government. Birds are my vice. When I get a few days off, or better still a few weeks, I'm apt to sneak away from town and leave my good wife to her various social engagements. The bottom lands and the river bluffs are the best places in the state for bird life. Up here I see no one but birds and the unique Valley Farms household.'

'You have a house near Mr. Gladstone's?' she asked. 'How nice! Then perhaps I'll be seeing you.'

'You'll be seeing me tonight at dinner,' he said, 'than which for me nothing could be nicer. But one can hardly call my little hide-out a house, especially when you compare it with Valley Farms which is almost a feudal estate. All I possess is a one-room shack near the top of a small bluff, overlooking the river. But there is a fine view, so perhaps you'll drop in on me sometime. I'm not more than a mile from the big house.'

'I'd love to!' she exclaimed. 'Perhaps I could bring June along. '

'June too, of course,' he said, 'if she would care to come. She has never done me that honour so far. June's a rather queer child, I think Felix will agree, but I have never found her dull. I think your visit may be interesting, Miss Archer. I hope it may be happy – or at any rate profitable.

Of course out here we're very remote; it's a little world of its own. I'm sure at any rate that it will be a new kind of experience for you.'

'Now, Professor,' Felix exclaimed, 'you're talking as if Miss Archer was about to bury herself in the African jungle. Don't let him scare you, Miss Archer. He's got quite an imagination, the professor has.'

And suddenly Kate remembered the strange note that was in her purse. The nervousness, the doubt she had felt alone in her bedroom swept over her again with a qualm as of seasickness. Because in her room there was still time to retreat: she need not, after all, have answered the knock on the door; she could have written Mr. Gladstone that she had changed her mind; but now that she had started it was too late. She felt as if she were in one of the little cars on a roller coaster. It was slowly pulling her up the long slant to the dizzying take-off; at any moment the plunge would begin, and she could not get out; she could not stop the car; she could only draw in her breath and close her eyes tight, and swear never to get trapped in such a thing again.

Then she was glad this feeling had come back, because obviously the way to strip the note of its mystery was to tell Mr. Hatfield about it, Mr. Hatfield and Felix: it would be no longer a secret, no longer something buried in her mind, but a trivial objective fact of common knowledge.

'I've had a new experience already', she said. 'Not very important but it sort of worried me a little. You'll probably think I'm foolish.'

Professor Hatfield cocked his eye at her, and leaned forward as a robin might do if he thought he saw a worm. 'I'm sure not', he said. 'What is it?'

Kate opened her purse, took out the note and handed it to him. He stared at it for a long minute with his lashes drawn together. 'Hmmm-hmmm' he muttered at last, in a tone that reminded her of Dr. Medway whenever he examined her teeth. 'Have you told Felix about this?'

'I've told nobody. It arrived in the two o'clock mail this afternoon.'

The reassuring laugh she had expected did not come; Professor Hatfield's expression remained thoughtful, and the beauty of these wild hills seemed all at once faintly poisonous, as if the region were enchanted.

'May I tell him about it?' the professor asked.

She tried to laugh. 'Of course. Why not? You don't think it means anything?'

'Listen, Felix', Professor Hatfield said. 'What do you think of this? DON'T GO TO MR. GLADSTONE'S. YOU'LL BE SORRY IF YOU DO. Sort of an ominous start for poor Miss Archer's visit, isn't it?'

'It looks to me,' Felix said, 'like some kind of a joke; but if it is, it's a damn poor one. You'll excuse my language, I hope.'

'A joke? Hmmm . . .' The professor squinted as if he were peering into the future. 'Well, very possibly. And now, Felix, if you'll let me out at the top of the next hill, I'll coast down the lane to the foot of my bluff.'

In a minute the car stopped again and Felix was lifting out the bicycle as neatly as he had lifted it in.

'There's Valley Farms', Professor Hatfield said, pointing down the long steep hill ahead of them. 'You get the best view of the estate from here. I'm over there to the left, beyond those woods.'

'How perfectly lovely!' Kate exclaimed, and for a moment she forgot everything in the charm of the view.

Directly below them was a huge green bowl, chequered with woods and fields, and cut in two by the white line of the highway. To the left of the road there clustered a group of red-roofed buildings, surrounded by shrubberies, by gardens and lawns – the whole thing shining in the midafternoon light with a strange liquid clearness as if you were staring down at it through still water.

Professor Hatfield got out of the car and shook Kate's hand.

'I'll be seeing you tonight then', he said.

He took his bicycle from Felix, swung his foot over the bar, and turned back to give her one more of his shrewd glances. 'Perhaps I should explain,' he added, 'that it wasn't just the wording of your note that interested me. Had it occurred to you that the red crayon might be meant to suggest the idea of blood?'

Chapter Two

KATE waited on the front steps while Felix lifted out her bags. She had never seen a more charming house; its whole atmosphere was reassuring. It was of whitewashed brick long and low, with blue-shuttered french windows opening on to a grassy terrace. The lawn through which the driveway wound stretched for acres behind her, scattered with oaks, with birches, with huge pines, and beyond it, like a spectacular green wall, the wooded hills seemed to rise almost vertically to shut out the rest of the world. The air had a damp freshness down here which brought out sharply the smell of grass and leaves – perhaps because the river was so near.

She had noticed a whining and scratching from inside the door, and as Felix opened it a little black and white beagle dashed out, wriggled first around Felix's legs, then around hers, then flew circling over the lawn, its ears waving, its tail held high like a pennant.

'How perfectly darling!' she exclaimed. 'What's his name? How old is he?'

'It's a young lady', Felix said. 'Her name is Bobbie, and she's not quite five months old.'

Kate watched her with delight as she stopped so suddenly she fell all over herself, grabbed a large stick, dashed back to the door and dropped the stick at Kate's feet. Then with her chin on the ground between her front paws, her hindquarters raised, her tail wagging frantically, she looked up at Kate with dark liquid eyes. Kate could not resist stooping down. The little hound thrust its head between her outstretched hands, and Kate could feel through the silky skin the bones of her skull and jaw, as delicate and buoyant as those of a bird.

'I see you've made friends already', Felix said. 'Bobbie certainly has good taste.'

As Kate stood up she saw a woman in black with a maid's apron walking toward the door from the back of the wide hallway. She was middle-aged, with a weathered handsome face and thin brown hair pulled back from her forehead and temples.

'My wife', Felix explained to Kate. 'Ruby, my girl, let me present to you Miss Katherine Archer. Quite an addition to the household, if you ask me.'

'I didn't ask you', the woman said in such a fierce voice that it almost made Kate jump. For an instant she glared at Felix; then she shrugged her shoulders and peered at Kate.

'That outburst wasn't meant for you, Miss Archer', Felix apologized. 'It was meant for me, though I'm afraid you're partly to blame. Youth and beauty can be very disturbing as we grow older, can't they, Ruby, my love?'

Beneath the suavity of his tone there was a sudden hardness that Kate would not have expected: it seemed not so much Felix's own voice as a reflection of his wife's.

'Oh shut up!' the woman said; then as she turned to Kate her face lost something of its belligerence. 'I'm sorry, miss', she said. 'But Felix is right. It wasn't meant for you. We're a queer household here at the farm, and you might as well learn it now as later.'

'I'll take up your bags', Felix said. 'Don't let Ruby scare you, Miss Archer. Her bark is worse than her bite.'

Felix walked back through the hall to the stairway, and Kate looked over her shoulder to see where Bobbie had gone. At first she did not discover her; but then she saw her, through the still-open door, a small black and white object racing around a pine tree a hundred yards or more from the house.

'You better step in there', Ruby said, escorting her to a doorway on the right. 'Mr. Gladstone wants to talk to you before you see June. He's lying down. I'll go call him.'

Kate, who was apt to be critical of furniture arrangements, glanced sharply about the room. It was large and low-ceiled, its floor entirely covered with a sea-green carpet, which recalled her impression, as they had looked down from the hilltop, that the valley was under water. For its size, the room was sparsely furnished: there were several sofas and easy chairs; along the walls stood two or three carved chests like pieces she had seen in Brittany. Besides the three french windows opening on the terrace, there was a fourth one, at the further end, screened by a Venetian blind; and through the slats she could see another, smaller terrace, this one paved not with grass but with red tiles and strewn with wicker chairs and tables. Beyond it, in the sunlight, she caught the gleam of delphinium and scarlet lilies.

She thought of the grim woman who had just left her: perhaps Ruby, if she was as jealous of Felix as she seemed, had sent the note in a last effort to prevent the arrival of an attractive young girl in the house. 'But of course Ruby had never seen me', thought Kate, and then smiled at her own conceit. And yet, in fairness to herself, it was not really conceit: she had learned by experience that most men found her nice to look at, and it would be crazy to pretend that she did not know it and did not thoroughly enjoy it, even if it was sometimes embarrassing. Or again, perhaps Felix had sent it himself, for the sake of domestic peace, suspecting that Ruby would resent her coming. She wished that either one of these explanations was true; then everything would be cleared up and she would feel free to enjoy this wonderful place; but she was not convinced. She

couldn't believe it of Felix, and not even of Ruby. In spite
of her dourness, she looked honest and only too forthright.

As she strolled toward the farther window, Kate noticed
that a pair of feet was protruding from one of the wicker
chairs whose back was turned to the house. They were
small feet, wearing scarlet sandals with very high heels,
and through the straps Kate could see that the toe-nails
were painted crimson. Could that be Clotilde, she wondered: it was certainly not June. But then the thickness
of the ankles and the flabbiness of the bare calves, daubed
with sun tan, made her sure that this was an older woman.
It must be Mrs. Gladstone, June's mother, though one
wouldn't have thought it. A tall glass, empty except for a
sprig of mint, stood on the tiles beside her.

Then as Kate idly watched, an extraordinarily pretty
girl in grey flannel slacks appeared on the terrace from
somewhere behind the house. She had a small head set on
a long neck; she looked as composed, as beautifully made
up, as the models in a fashion display; but the most striking
thing about her was her hair, which floated down to her
shoulders in waves of the glossiest, palest gold that Kate
had ever seen. Kate thought regretfully of her own hair,
which had had that almost silvery brightness when she was
two or three (Mother had kept a lock of it), but which had
darkened ever since. She suspected that she would not like
this girl: she seemed far too smooth; but she did arouse
Kate's sporting instincts. It would be interesting to see
her fiancé.

'Well you owe me five dollars', Clotilde called to her
stepmother (Kate was sure she had identified them both).
'I beat him 6-4, 6-3.'

'Anyone else but you,' a throaty voice answered from
the chair, 'wouldn't feel right about taking the money. It's
quite obvious that if you did beat him it was only because
he let you.'

The first thing that struck Kate about this voice was the fact that, with its drawl, the mannered way it lingered on certain syllables, it assumed the presence of an audience. Since they were betting, Kate felt she would be willing to bet even money that Mrs. Gladstone had once been an actress.

'You ought to know Ralph by this time!' Clotilde laughed, and her tone seemed exaggeratedly casual, as if she were trying to underline its difference from the older woman's. 'He's not so damn chivalrous as all that.'

'Chivalrous!' Mrs. Gladstone snorted. 'Who said anything about chivalry? If he didn't bother to win, it was because he was bored, poor lamb, and God knows I don't blame him! You're not at your best, my dove, on the tennis court.'

The voices came through the open window as clearly as if they were in the room. Kate did not know what to do: should she cough, or pretend to adjust the blind? But it would be embarrassing to make her presence known now; and as far as Clotilde and Mrs. Gladstone were concerned, she felt they would not care in the least who might hear them.

Clotilde had walked nearer her stepmother's chair, and was gazing down at her with a fixed irritating smile.

'Mavis, darling,' she said, 'I'm afraid what really worries you is the idea, and I admit there's something in it, that it's *I* who am growing bored with *him*.'

'And why, pray, should that interest me?' Mavis sounded like a duchess on the stage of a summer theatre.

Clotilde lifted her fine eyebrows and drew her lips together in an expression of innocence. 'Ah, why indeed?' she asked.

'Darling, do you know what you remind me of?' Mrs. Gladstone went on after the slightest pause; and Kate was now aware of a rasping note beneath the smoothness of her voice. 'You make me think of a mosquito, a very charming, slim mosquito – that goes without saying – with lovely gauzy wings, but a mosquito nonetheless. And I'm terribly afraid, you know, that Ralph is beginning to agree with me.'

Clotilde seemed to be having a very good time. 'Let's see what *you* remind *me* of', she said. 'It's like that descriptive game, isn't it, and you have chosen the subject of insects. Of course it's very hard to think of you in such terms. If you had chosen flowers, say, or nice things to drink, nothing would have been easier. But if I had to describe you as an insect, I think I should be inclined to choose a tick, one of those pretty, plump little ticks you find on dogs.'

Mrs. Gladstone laughed huskily. 'I hope not a tick', she said. 'They can be quite dangerous, you know.'

'Not unless you let them get under your skin', Clotilde replied.

Mrs. Gladstone's laugh died away in a kind of purring chuckle. 'I don't flatter myself that I could ever get under yours', she said. 'It's – shall we say too fine-grained? So you're perfectly safe.'

Kate was amused but at the same time slightly revolted by this scrap of conversation; she felt at least that she was beginning to understand what Miss Barstow had meant when she said that June's family background left much to be desired. Then, the next instant, a young man in white flannels appeared on the terrace, and in her surprise and pleasure this malicious sparring seemed all at once unimportant. He was a solid straight young man, with chestnut hair, a brown skin, and deep-set brown eyes. His features were large; his eyebrows were almost ferociously dark and thick; but the general impression one gathered from his face was that of a somewhat detached and distinctly patient kindness. It was Ralph Green! There could be no doubt of it. What fun that he should be here! She remembered now that Felix had mentioned a Mr. Green, and of course Mavis had referred to 'Ralph'; but it had not occurred to Kate to put the two names together. She had not seen Ralph for five years and she thought of him always in connection with the summer she had spent in Maine. She had been only fifteen years old and Ralph must have been twenty-one or two; but he had taken her sailing, he had coached her in tennis; he had been kind, even affectionate, never in the least condescending; and Kate during the last month of her stay had been more nearly in love with him than she had ever been with anyone since that faraway summer.

Of course, to him, she had been just a rather big little girl; he had liked her very much; she could realize that he must sometimes have been amused by her. She would always be grateful to him because she felt that he had given her a standard of comparison by which she could judge the series of younger boys who had begun that very winter to fall in love with her. She could hardly wait now to speak to him. She wondered if he, too, would be surprised; she even wondered if he would remember her. Then like a chill it came over her that Ralph was engaged to marry this awful Clotilde.

'I couldn't find the last ball', he said, and there was an edge to his voice, suggesting that even his patience had its limits. 'I'm not going to waste any more time looking for it.'

'Now really, Ralph!' Clotilde exclaimed. 'They were very special ones. It's almost impossible to get them.'

Ralph looked at her with a fixed and quite unrevealing smile. 'You like things that are hard to get, don't you?' he said. 'You like things made to order. I wonder if there's anything you'd enjoy, if you thought that the average person, the common run-of-the-mill individual, could get it just as easily as you could.'

Ralph was standing very straight and yet he seemed quite relaxed; he had the surprising light stance and poise that you notice sometimes in even the most dignified and massive dogs. Kate watched him with keen curiosity. He was not so handsome as she remembered him; no actual young man could be that. In fact, she had to confess, he was not handsome at all; and yet it seemed to her that she liked his face more than ever. Its present impatience or irony, or even scorn, seemed only to emphasize what must be its habitual gentleness. You felt that he had learned not to expect too much either from himself or others, but that he was more inclined to be tolerant of others than of himself. Clotilde met his eyes.

'I haven't given the matter much thought', she said coolly.

'No, I expect not', he said. 'Well, I'm going up to take a shower. See you at dinner.'

He stepped out of sight toward the front of the house, and Kate felt with pleasure that he had snubbed Clotilde; already she had the sense that she was watching some kind of game and that the side she was cheering had just won a point. A moment later she could hear him opening the front door and running upstairs. She had almost gone out into the hall to waylay him; but then she thought it would be more fun to surprise him at dinner, and she would have hated to do anything that might have seemed like thrusting herself on his attention before he noticed her.

A faint noise made her look around, and she saw a large dark man in a Palm Beach suit, with a rose in his buttonhole – a man whom she thought she had seen somewhere before – coming toward her across the watery expanse of carpet.

'Were the girls out there putting on one of their little shows?' he asked in a deep voice with a slightly sardonic intonation.

Kate blushed. She felt like a child caught in a preserve closet. 'Well, I don't know', she said. 'They *were* talking and I'm afraid I couldn't help —'

The man grinned, and his teeth looked younger and more vigorous than the rest of his face. 'Of course you couldn't and why should you? I only hope they kept the script clean.'

He held out an enormous hairy hand, and as she took it she realized why he seemed familiar: in spite of the pouches beneath his eyes, the sag of his jowls, his nearly bald head, he reminded her of June. He had the same oblong face with its heavy chin and small rounded nose, the same swarthiness of skin, the same dark glance; and yet his face, at any rate when he spoke, had a kind of concentration, of liveliness, in spite of its air of fatigue, which June's had always lacked. He was an ugly man, but she could imagine that he might be interesting, even attractive.

'I'm sorry I kept you waiting', he went on. 'All the more so, now that I've seen you. The fact is I was napping in my underwear, and I didn't feel I knew you quite well enough to appear as I was. June told me you were beautiful, but I knew she had a crush on you – in a perfectly nice way, of course – so I made considerable allowance. But my word!' – He looked her up and down with embarrassingly direct admiration beneath his bantering air. 'It was really an understatement.'

Once more she saw his lopsided grin. 'You may give quite a jolt to Clotilde,' he went on, 'and poor old Mavis will be sick; but what a treat for Ralph and Jo, not to speak of my aged self! And I mustn't forget Felix. Felix was quite a lady's man in his prime, the rascal. Don't let that respectful manner fool you. I bet Felix was licking his lips!'

Kate felt that Mr. Gladstone spoke as if she were a

choice morsel to be served up at dinner. She suspected that he was trying to tease her and determined to show no sign that she noticed it.

'I'm looking forward to seeing June again', she said. 'She must have changed a good deal in the last four years.'

Mr. Gladstone sent her a sharp glance. 'The more, the better, eh?'

If she hadn't prepared herself against confusion, Kate might have blushed. 'I didn't mean that at all,' she said, 'and I think you talk horridly for a father. I noticed it in your letter too.'

He looked at her quizzically and as she met his gaze she had the feeling that he liked her all the more for her sharp retort.

'I know my appearance suggests one of the larger an-thropoid apes,' he said after an instant, 'but that doesn't mean I don't have a father's heart. But wait a minute —'

He walked past her over to the window that opened on to the terrace. 'You see, the theatre had reversed itself', he explained. 'We had become the stage in here, and Mavis and Clotilde had become the audience.' He raised the blind and closed the casement window. 'That's better,' he said, 'and now please sit down. I don't know why I didn't suggest it before. Let's say it was because I was dazzled.'

Kate sat down in one of the big leather chairs near the fireplace; it gave her the same feeling of super-comfort that the seat in the car had done. Mr. Gladstone seated himself in an even larger chair on the other side of the hearth, leaned back and crossed one ankle over his knee.

'Seriously, Miss Archer, I'm damn glad you're here', he said. 'But I'm not going to call you that. Katherine? Kate? Kate's what they call you, isn't it?'

'Most of my friends call me Kate', she admitted.

'Swell! Anyhow: to be frank, I feel just a little bit guilty

about June, as I told you in my letter. Of course she's not
much more decorative than I am, though I will say she
has improved during the last year, and I suspect you can
give her some damn good advice. You know, her clothes,
her hair, and things like that. I think she's really a nice kid.
Between ourselves, I think she's worth two of Clotilde. I
confess I have a weakness for Clotilde, but I know damn
well it's mostly because she's such a knockout to look at.
Clotilde knows what she wants and she'll get it, regard-
less. It may be my fault for spoiling her, but her mother
was very much the same type. When I was a young man
I was a lousy judge of women, at least the ones I married.
But to go back to poor June. I hope you will stay here for
a month anyway; and if you can give her a little self-
confidence and brighten her up a bit, you'll have done
your good deed for the year. We're a pretty free and easy
bunch out here, as you're probably discovering, but I
think you'll live through it. If you can stand me, you ought
to be able to take the rest of us, and you seem to be doing
pretty well so far.'

A scurrying in the hall made Kate turn her head in time
to see Bobbie dash into the room, slide back on her
haunches for a moment in the midst of her rush, to look
around her, and then make for Kate's ankles with a series
of little grunts and barks. Kate put down her hands to
protect her stockings, and Bobbie, after a few growling
charges, wheeled on her hind legs, her front paws waving,
her ears swirling about her face like the curls of a bal-
lerina, and dashed straight across the room for another
arm-chair. Kate thought she was going to fling herself
against it, but in the nick of time, without slackening her
speed, she flattened herself out and half slid, half scrambled
under the border of pleated chintz that touched the floor.
Then almost at once her head appeared peeking from
under the edge, her chin pressed close against the carpet,

while her eyes gleamed up at Kate as if to challenge her
to try to drag her out of this refuge.

'Bobbie, come here! Bobbie, where are you?'

It was June's voice, and the next instant she stepped into
the room and came toward Kate with a smile that showed
her large strong teeth. At the same time Bobbie's head
ducked under the chair, and then she scrambled out,
holding in her mouth a very dirty doll made of string,
which she brought over and dropped at Kate's feet. But
Kate had hardly time to notice her now, because she was
so curious to see what June would be like as a 'young
girl'.

June shook her hand vigorously, leaned toward her as
if to kiss her, and then straightened up as if she did not
quite dare.

'Kate!' she exclaimed in her rather deep voice, which
had always been the most attractive thing about her. 'It's
the same old Katey! I was so afraid you might have
changed. I was so afraid you might seem all grown-up and
fancy, but you don't look any different.'

It was not quite the same old June, Kate realized at
once. Not only was she about a foot taller, several inches
taller than Kate now, but she was far less stolid-looking.
She still moved with awkward abruptness; her face was
still too heavy, but it had a kind of intensity of expression,
a liveliness at this minute of greeting, which suggested
her father more than ever. Her complexion, too, dark and
slightly oily, was at any rate much better than it had been.
At present she was wearing too much lipstick of too pink
a shade; her black hair fluffed in unbecoming wisps about
her cheeks; and Kate who liked nothing better than fixing
things over according to her own very particular taste,
looked forward, as her father had suggested, to starting
in at once on the reconstruction of her appearance. June,
with a little tact and care, might be smart-looking, even

distinguished. Kate was sure Mr. Gladstone had been right when he said she was worth two of Clotilde.

'It's great fun to be seeing you again', Kate said. 'It doesn't seem as if it could be four years since we were together, except that you certainly have grown up, if I haven't. And this is such a lovely place! I've never seen anything like it. You must show me all around. I'm sure we'll have a wonderful summer, June.'

'June, sweet,' Mr. Gladstone said, with a touch of irony in his tone, which probably, Kate thought, had become so habitual that he was no longer aware of it, 'I suggest that the first thing you show Kate is her own room. Felix took up her bags. And then she may doubtless want to be left in peace to unpack.'

'I'd love to have June help me unpack', said Kate. 'That is, if she wants to.'

'You bet I want to', June said. 'I'm crazy to see your clothes. You always had such pretty clothes.'

'Well then, my little dears,' Mr. Gladstone said, making only a token gesture as if to rise from his chair, 'I'll be seeing you before dinner.'

As the two girls walked upstairs side by side, Bobbie climbed ahead of them, putting first her two front feet on each step above her and then bringing up her hind-quarters with a little bounce and jerk that made Kate think of a mechanical rabbit. At the top of the stairs they turned to the left along a pleasant hall, with green and white straw matting on the floor, and then turned to the right into another wing which led toward the back of the house.

Presently they reached the end of the corridor. 'Here we are', June said. 'Your room will be this one straight ahead, and mine is here to the left. They're next to each other.'

Kate pushed eagerly through the door into her room,

3

and then couldn't help smiling because she loved it so. On the floor there was the same green and white matting, whose damp smell reminded her of Matunuck. The chintz curtains had a pattern of cornflowers and poppies, and near the bed stood a luxurious chaise-longue.

'It's not so big,' June said, 'but I've always liked this room. I used to wish it was mine, but I couldn't have it because it was used as a guest room. Do you like it, Kate?'

'I just love it!' Kate said. 'I can't imagine a nicer room.'

She walked gaily across to one of the windows. 'And what a pretty view!' she exclaimed. 'It looks so quaint and peaceful.'

An oblong of turf, like a bowling green, stretched smoothly to a little house of white brick, with mossy red tiles and blue shutters like the main building; but this was as miniature and dainty as a cottage in a fairy tale. Behind it a wall of trees rose so steeply that she had to lean out of the window to look up at the sky. And from the little house she could hear the sound of a violin.

'I suppose that's Mr. – I suppose that's Jo', she said. 'Felix told me about him.'

'Yes, that's Jo', June said, and if Felix's tone had suggested disapproval, June's expressed real dislike. 'He lives out there so his practising won't disturb us, but sometimes when he plays late at night it keeps me awake. Mavis, that's mother, accompanies him; she plays pretty well; but lately it's been mostly Clotilde. She plays too.'

Kate smiled. 'You don't think much of him, do you?' she said. 'Felix didn't seem to either, not that he wasn't very polite. What's wrong with him?'

'Nothing's wrong with him really,' June said after a minute, 'except that he's a sponge. I don't blame *him* so much. He's no worse than the rest of them.' And then her face darkened into a scowl, the kind of scowl Kate remem-

bered when girls at school had bothered to tease her. 'It's
just that it's all so nasty. Everything's nasty around here.
It's always been that way ever since I can remember. It's
not fair for things to be so nasty!'

Her face suddenly lightened, and she looked with the
new intensity of her glance directly at Kate. 'That's one of
the reasons I wanted you to come', she said. 'Because you
won't mind it, I guess. It's not *your* family.'

At that moment Kate was so sorry for her that she felt
like putting her arms around her and kissing her, but it
might be just as well not to start a precedent. She wondered if she were referring to any special things. Whatever
they were, she was perhaps exaggerating.

'We can treat everything like an adventure', she said.
'And we won't have to bother with people when we don't
want to.'

'But Kate', June went on after a minute, in a new tone
of voice, no longer passionate but rather stilted and hesitant. 'That's not the only reason I'm glad you've come.
That's not the main reason.'

'What is it?' Kate asked curiously.

When June spoke, her voice was almost a whisper. 'The
main reason is that I'm afraid.'

Kate felt a crawling sensation inside her stomach, as if
the roller coaster had begun its downward plunge, but
she tried to smile incredulously. 'Afraid!' she exclaimed.
'What on earth are you afraid of?'

'You mustn't laugh', June said. 'It's not my imagination. Listen, Kate. A week ago I was walking with Bobbie
on the river bluffs. I walk around here a lot. I always have.
That hill out there behind the little house is the start of a
bluff. It rises for just a few hundred yards, getting steeper
and steeper, and then there are rocks, and the bluff drops
almost straight down into the river. It's quite wild all along
the shore. The bluffs go on for miles, and there are lots of

little nooks and caves. I guess nobody knows them all, unless it's Professor Hatfield. Felix said you met him on the way out here. Well, on one of the bluffs about a mile down the river from here, Bobbie started barking and barking. I thought it was at some animal so I began to explore. Over the crest in a kind of steep place I found a little cave I'd never noticed, because a juniper tree spread out from the bank right smack above it. It was sort of hard to get down, but I'm a pretty good climber, and inside there was an old blanket and some whisky bottles and an electric torch and a kind of tin lunch box that I didn't look into. Bobbie was still yelping on top of the bluff, because she couldn't get down, and all at once I had the most awful creepy feeling that someone was near. I don't think I heard anyone. I didn't see anyone. It was just a feeling, but it was so awful I could hardly climb back around the juniper.'

'I can imagine that', Kate exclaimed. 'I'd have never dared climb down in the first place. I suppose it was just some camper. Or perhaps a hunter, if anything's in season.'

'I don't think it was an ordinary camper', June said.

'But why not?' Kate asked. It almost scared her to feel such relief that June's fear was irrational: what had she been expecting anyway?

'Wait a minute', June said. 'I'll be right back.' And she hurried out of the room.

Kate wouldn't have believed how empty June's absence would make it seem. Even Bobbie lying beside the bed, her slim hind legs spread backward like a frog's, was scarcely a consolation. She could still hear the violin, but it only increased the silence of everything else. That wall of trees seemed now rather suffocating, as if it shut out the natural air and light. Thank heaven, at least, that Ralph was here! She gave a faint start as June came back into the room, just as she had started several hours ago (it seemed like an entirely different day) when Felix had knocked at her door back in town.

Then as June handed her a letter, her heart began to beat so violently that it was almost an agony to force herself to smile. Because she recognized that envelope, that printing.

'It came in the mail just two days later', June said. 'That was five days ago.'

Kate felt that she could not trust her voice. She took out the paper, and there printed in the same red crayon – blood-red it looked to her now – she saw the following message:

IF YOU GO ON POKING YOUR NOSE INTO THINGS, YOU'LL BE SORRY. AND I MEAN SORRY!

Chapter Three

WHEN Kate looked out of her bedroom door at ten minutes to seven, she was glad to see that June's door was still closed. She had planned to start this very first night with June's hair, with a general reclaiming process, but the more she thought over this new red-printed warning, the more anxious she was to tell Ralph about it; and she would prefer doing this when June was not present.

Kate had not told June about her own letter; there had seemed to be no point in increasing her nervousness. Yet perhaps she ought to tell June; she had proof now at any rate that the writer of the notes was a person associated with this region; this second letter made the whole affair seem much more ominous, and she felt that she could not sleep tonight until she had asked Ralph's advice. She only hoped that she might have a chance to speak to him before June came down.

She had thought regretfully, as June showed her about the farm, how much she would have enjoyed everything if only the air had not been tainted by this clammy breath of the mysterious. It kept seeping in around the edges of her mind to ruin her pleasure in this beautiful, faraway place. It was like a symptom that you half suspect may point to some horrible disease, and that all the while your common sense tells you is probably of no importance: at one instant, desperately, you are sure that your life is threatened; at the next, you are merely annoyed with your jumpy nerves.

In spite of its name, Kate felt that Mr. Gladstone's home was more of a country estate than a farm. The buildings, like the house, were of whitewashed brick; none of them was large, and among them were little gravelled court-yards leading one out of another, with espaliered fruit trees trained in angular patterns against the white walls. June had shown her the two riding horses in the stable; then they had seen the garage, where Felix was polishing the green convertible, and the cow barn, where Olaf Larson, an old Norwegian, was milking a Guernsey cow. June took Kate to a cottage across the paddock to call on Emmy, his wife. Both of them had been on the place, June explained, since before her father went to college, and they still spoke with a Norwegian accent. Then June and she had walked through the formal garden, of which Kate had already caught a glimpse between the slats of the blind; they had skirted the tennis court and the kitchen garden, while Bobbie kept running off to explore and returning to bounce about their legs. A light at once blue and iridescent had begun to fill the shadows; and eastward, beyond the lawn and the fields, the wooded hills through which she had driven three hours ago looked, in their soft brilliance, more impenetrable than ever.

Kate was very much pleased with June. As this awkward girl felt the noses of the horses and stroked the sides of the cows, there had been a brusque grace and directness in her movements. She had seemed thoroughly at home with animals: no doubt she loved them more than she did people, although she had shown something of this easy manner toward Felix and the Larsons. This struck Kate as rather pathetic in its suggestion that she knew these workers about the place more intimately than she knew her own family.

As they were entering the house, by way of the kitchen, June said: 'I'd have loved to take you up the bluff and show you the river. That's the nicest thing around here, but I don't know – I kind of felt perhaps we'd better not.'

'It must be nearly dinnertime', Kate said lightly. There was no point in letting June suspect how much she would have hated just then to plunge into those woods behind the house.

She walked swiftly now along the halls, down the broad stairs and into the living-room. It was empty, but the blinds at the end were drawn up, the french window was open, and she could see a man in a white suit standing alone on the terrace. For a minute she thought it might be Ralph, but then as she crossed the room she noticed that this man's hair was black; he must be Jo Martinez, the violinist.

She was hesitating in the middle of the room, wondering whether to join him or wait until someone else appeared, when he turned and saw her.

'Hullo', he called. 'Come on out! Don't be afraid. I'm quite harmless.' His voice was resonant and he spoke with a marked accent.

Kate came forward willingly; she was curious to see what this man was like. 'You must be Mr. Martinez', she said, as she stepped out on to the terrace. 'I'm Kate Archer.'

'Kate!' he exclaimed. 'One of those simple English names that can either be so commonplace or can be filled with so much beauty! Kate and Jo! My name is José but all my American friends call me Jo, and I'm sure – I was sure the first instant that I saw you, in a flash, like that! – that we should be friends.'

'That wasn't very long ago', she said smiling.

Felix and June had prepared her for someone at once sleek and forbidding, but this man suggested neither a thug nor a gigolo. He was wiry, even darker than Mr. Gladstone, with shining hair brushed straight back from a very low forehead; his face, without being handsome, was aquiline and alert; the intensity of his eyes made her think of a Goya portrait.

'It seems already that for me a long time has passed since then', he said. 'Or perhaps I should say the element of time is not involved. When the saints saw visions they entered a world that is timeless. Not that I am a saint – please don't let me give you that impression!'

'I'm sure you're far too young to be a saint', Kate said. 'Perhaps you will be sometime.'

The man beamed at her but shook his head. 'Ah, ah!' he exclaimed. 'And I thought you were so innocent, so artless, I who pride myself on reading human nature. Yet you have the wisdom of the serpent. You see at a glance that after I have exhausted my passion for this world I might well conceive a passion for the next; and you also put your finger on my leading vanity: the desire to remain, to appear young, especially before beautiful women. It's disconcerting a little, because you would not have sensed that vanity if you had not also seen that I am not so young as I should like to appear.'

As a matter of fact, Kate guessed that he was in his late twenties. It was pleasant and gay, at the end of this dis- quieting afternoon, to be talking nonsense with an at- tractive young man, even if he was rather exotic. She realized that her comfortable sense of having Ralph in reserve, as it were, made her feel more kindly toward Jo, whose strangeness might otherwise have faintly repelled her. She was delighted that she had put on her white organdie and that she had brushed her hair until it gleamed and floated about her shoulders, almost as soft, though not so silvery, as Clotilde's. It was with Clotilde in mind that she had tried to make herself appear as young as possible, that she had chosen such a candid-looking dress and been quite sparing with her lipstick. Since she could not hope to equal her sophistication, the best she could do was to suggest by contrast that Clotilde was brittle and over- worldly.

'And you have put your finger on *my* weakness too', she said. 'I think I'm the one to be embarrassed.'

'Then it must have been my little finger,' he exclaimed, 'and it was quite by accident. What is your weakness? There are few things I enjoy so much as having lovely women tell me their weaknesses.'

'I'm sure you must have had lots of experience in that line', she said.

He shrugged his shoulders. 'What will you have? I'm humble. I'm sympathetic. I'm indulgent. If I could only behave myself, I would have made an excellent priest.'

Before Kate could think of some phrase about her own love of flattery, she was startled by a throaty chuckle from the living-room, and turning her head she saw a woman who surely must be Mavis standing on the threshold of the terrace. Kate was intensely curious to meet the person who went with the voice she had heard this afternoon.

Mrs. Gladstone was small, and not so much plump as baggy. She was wearing a kind of tea gown of cream-coloured lace which trailed on the floor behind her but flared open in front to show her legs to the knee and at-tract attention to her feet, still stockingless, and humped into tiny mesh sandals with even higher heels than the red ones which Kate had seen. Across the room her face might still appear pretty, with the fleshy dated prettiness of a Sennett bathing beauty; but as near as this it looked as if it were made of wax which had been kept in too warm a place: the nose was beginning to spread, the cheeks and chin to sag, and about the eyes, the mouth, the throat, a network of wrinkles now filled with powder suggested to Kate the fine veins of a leaf. Her lips, painted rather crookedly, were wine-coloured, her eyelids were cerulean blue, and a cloud of brassy hair stood out like a synthetic halo around her head.

'José,' she exclaimed with a guttural Spanish *J*, 'did I

hear you tell this poor child that you'd make a good priest?
God pity the woman who trusted herself to your ghostly
administrations!'

'Oh, I don't know', he said airily. 'Even as a layman
I've managed to bring comfort to some poor souls.'

Mrs. Gladstone advanced toward Kate with a jerky
sway that just missed being a hobble. 'And so you're
Kate', she said. 'Poor little June has raved about you,
and really I don't wonder. I hope this depraved and
utterly decadent young man here hasn't been telling you
some of his "feelthy stories".'

'Mavis, my love,' Jo said, 'I save those for ears that I
think will enjoy them.'

At this moment June and Clotilde stepped out of the
living-room, side by side yet certainly not together, with
Mr. Gladstone close behind them. June was wearing a
bunchy pink dress that made her look her worst, while
Clotilde was in sleek pale-grey silk, the colour of a sea-
gull's wing; her dress was so inconspicuous and yet so striking that Kate was sure it must be the work of some famous
designer. Around her long throat was a string of pearls.

Mr. Gladstone grinned at Kate, with the left corner of
his mouth pulled down as if it were holding an invisible
cigar.

'Charming, my dear! Charming!' he exclaimed. 'You
strike a completely new note in our menagerie.' And Kate
felt a little as if a large and aged grisly bear, pressing close
to the front of its cage, had shown signs of wanting to play
with her through the bars.

'But you and Clotilde haven't met each other yet', he
went on. 'One can hardly expect two such beautiful girls
to like each other, but that's no reason why you shouldn't
be dear friends.'

While he was speaking Clotilde had given her a level
glance, and now she came forward with her hand out-

stretched and with a smile that even Kate had to admit was charming. If she had not heard her this afternoon with her stepmother, she would not have guessed how very unpleasant she could be – and perhaps with Mavis there was some excuse. She wondered if Ralph so far had caught a glimpse of Clotilde's other manner. Poor Ralph!

'I'm so glad you've come', Clotilde exclaimed. 'For June's sake, and also for my own. I'm sure we can have lots of fun.'

'I'm sure we can', Kate said; and as she took her hand, meeting her eyes with what she hoped was a look of spontaneous pleasure, she knew that Mr. and Mrs. Gladstone, that Jo and even June were all watching them. Inside her there was a small warm feeling of triumph, because she was sure Clotilde had come prepared to snub her, in a polite Park Avenue way, and then, seeing her, had simply not quite dared. This stranger, she must have thought, was too attractive not to be welcomed with complete friendliness; because any other treatment might be interpreted as an admission of inferiority.

Kate was glad, however, that just then Felix appeared from around the corner of the house with a large tray of cocktails and canapés. She would not have known what to say next to Clotilde; Clotilde showed no signs of speaking herself, and they could not have smiled at each other much longer. Then as Felix began passing the tray, Kate noticed Professor Hatfield walking toward them through the garden. Everyone was here now but Ralph.

An insinuating voice spoke close to her ear:

'A cocktail, Miss Kate? And how about a canapé? Those black ones are the best. I've sampled them.'

Felix stood at her elbow with the tray. He was leaning forward, the picture of the well-trained servant, but his eye was raised to catch hers with a look that seemed almost of complicity, of encouragement, and she could not have

sworn that his right eyelid had not flickered. She hoped
people did not notice the smile she gave him, because it
was so much more natural than the one she had given
Clotilde.

Professor Hatfield came over to speak to her, but she
hardly heard what he said, because at that moment Ralph
stepped out of the house and started to pour himself a
cocktail by the table where Felix left the tray. He raised
his glass, looked around him perfunctorily, and then as his
warm brown eye caught hers it was as if a light had been
turned on somewhere in the depths of his mind and was
illumining his whole face.

'Kate!' he exclaimed. 'Little Kate Archer! What on
earth are you doing here? This is wonderful! I can't
believe it.'

As she met his straight glance, at once so bright and so
deep, so gentle, and yet in the midst of all this strangeness
so completely reliable, she wondered how she ever could
have lost the sense of its special quality. It was like your
first whiff of the soft salt air after you have been for months
away from the sea. Then she blushed as she realized that
everyone was staring at her.

'Do you know Ralph?' June asked, and there was reproach in her voice. 'Why didn't you tell me, Katey?'

Kate tried to laugh. 'I only discovered it *was* Ralph a
little while ago', she said. 'I hadn't seen him for five years,
and I thought I wouldn't tell anybody until I was sure he
remembered me. It was just my vanity, I guess.'

Ralph crossed the terrace and seized her outstretched
hand.

'Remember you!' he said. 'Don't be silly! Do you think
I could forget that summer of ours? As a matter of fact,
I'm one of those stupid people that never forget anything.
It's pretty much of a curse as a rule, because most things
I'd much rather forget, but it does have its compensations.

When something happens I really want to remember, I've got it tucked away for life. I always hoped I'd run into you again, but I never thought it would be around here. Of course I heard June talking about "Kate", but I don't think she ever mentioned your last name.'

Clotilde laughed. 'Perhaps we should all withdraw,' she suggested, 'and give these two old friends a chance to talk over their memories.'

As Ralph glanced at his fiancée, Kate noticed again the fixed and blank smile with which he had faced her, out here, this afternoon.

'I'm going to do my best to see that we find plenty of chances', he said. 'You can certainly count on that.'

Kate was pleased by the finality in his voice; it was as if he were merely stating a fact that required no special emphasis. Then he continued to herself, but so quietly that only June and the professor, who were standing close beside them, could hear him:

'I might not have recognized you at that. In fact the more I look at you, the more surprised I am that I did. You were an exceptionally pretty little girl, Kate, but you've grown to be so beautiful! Or were you always that way and is it just that my taste has matured? How old were you at Hancock Point? Thirteen? Fourteen?'

'I was fifteen', she said with a pretence of indignation. 'I'm sorry if I seemed such a child. I was only a year younger than June is now.'

The other people had turned their attention elsewhere. Clotilde was talking and laughing with Jo; and Kate felt that she must bring June into the conversation.

'But June is so big', he said. 'You were just a little thing.'

'I'm not so terribly big', June said, and Kate could see that her feelings were hurt. 'I've lost eight pounds in the last two months.'

Kate put her arm around June's waist. 'He only means that you seem quite grown-up', she said, 'and when Ralph knew me in Maine I was just a skinny little girl.'

If it was reassuring to find Ralph here, it certainly did not diminish her sense of strangeness: the nicer he was, the queerer and the more illogical it seemed to think of him in Clotilde's clutches. It was like the kind of dream in which you find that you yourself are engaged, or possibly married, to someone whom you cannot bear; you can't imagine how it happened; you are simply faced with the fact and there is no escape.

She had sipped half her cocktail, which tasted of absinthe, and she was sure it must be very strong, because already the voices seemed louder and more confused, the colours more intense. The garden was completely shadowed by the hill behind the house, but the larkspur, the iris, the poppies, seemed to glow each with its own inner brightness among the paths and the watery green edgings, while the upper sky, above the bowl of the hills, shimmered in a dust of light. She could smell the lilies from here, or perhaps it was the clove pinks; it might even be the perfume that Mavis or Clotilde was wearing. She chattered of she hardly knew what with Ralph, with June, with Professor Hatfield; and everyone's features – their eyebrows, their noses, their mouths – looked exaggerated and somehow fixed in spite of their mobility. Her own must have that same strange look, and she felt she must control her smile and made an effort to speak softly. It seemed all at once like the world through the Looking Glass, but a Wonderland in which Alice's dream might change without warning into a grotesque kind of nightmare.

They must have remained on the terrace for more than half an hour. She drank her cocktail as slowly as she could, but she had finished long ago and with difficulty prevented first Jo and then Mr. Gladstone from refilling her glass, before they began to move into the dining-room. She was thankful she had taken no more, when Mavis seated her between Ralph and Mr. Hatfield. Perhaps during dinner she could tell Ralph about the letters.

At first, however, Mavis, who sat at his other side and whom Kate suspected of being quite tipsy, questioned him with vague repetitious innuendo about his former friendship with Kate. It was not until their soup bowls had been removed and Ruby had begun passing the chicken that Mavis, turning to Jo, who was seated on her other side, gave Kate a chance to talk with Ralph.

He leaned toward her at once, and as she met his eyes, peering warmly into her face from under his pirate's eyebrows, she had again the feeling which had come over her in the moment of his first recognition: that he had somehow shut her off with himself in a world that excluded all the rest of these strange people. Then, though his expression hardly changed, though his smile continued, it was as if a film had been drawn across his clear brown glance; they were once more, the two of them, breathing the air of this candle-lit dining-room, the same air as Mavis and Jo and Mr. Gladstone, an air that was at once too heavy and too thin.

'Ralph!' she exclaimed quickly, in an effort to recapture her sense of the instant before. 'Tell me what you've been doing. Tell me something about yourself.'

He shrugged his shoulders. 'What an unappetizing topic,' he said, 'to bring up at the dinner table!'

Beneath the lightness of his tone, behind the deliberate blankness of his eyes, she was suddenly aware of something tense, and it seemed to her even tortured; she realized that to know Ralph well one would have to be able, at times, to peer through the most opaque of shutters. She could hardly resist the impulse to place her fingers on his arm.

'I'm not just talking', she said gently. 'I wouldn't have asked what you've been doing, if I didn't really want to know.'

'The over-all answer to your question,' he said, 'would be "Nothing" – at least nothing of any consequence. As a matter of fact, until a month ago, I was working in the Bell Telephone Laboratories in New York. I'm relieved from that now, just hanging around for my navy commission to come through.'

'How exciting!' she said, and hoped the interest in her face might counteract the banality of her words. 'Will you like being in the Navy?'

'I think so,' he said, 'as much as anything. More than most things, I suppose. You know, it's strange', he went on; and she felt that his glance was growing transparent once more; there was a queer eagerness in his voice, as if for a long time he had found it impossible to talk, to talk as he would really like, to anyone – 'It's strange, but when war broke out, I was glad I wouldn't have to go. I was willing to do all I could, of course. I was no pacifist. But at the same time I felt I was very lucky to be in electronics. It seemed to me I could help the war effort most by staying just where I was. As a matter of fact, I think that was true. I'll probably make a lousy officer. I'll be doing a very special type of work, of course, but I think I could work better in a laboratory than on a ship.'

'Then why did you want to change?' she asked him.

She felt that some of the others, that especially Clotilde, might be watching them, might be wondering what they were saying; but the round table was large and dim; Mr. Gladstone, in jovial mood, was telling risqué stories to the general company. Ralph and she were talking in such low voices that at least no one could make out their words, and Kate just then, perhaps because of her cocktail, did not care what anyone thought.

'I hardly know why I changed', Ralph answered her. 'Partly vanity, no doubt, and a kind of envy. When I read of what was going on in the Pacific and across Europe, when I got letters from my friends with the Army or Navy, frankly, I couldn't help feeling somehow that I was in a theatre and much too far away from the stage. I wanted to grab one of the best seats, if I could. And then it must have been partly stubbornness. When I suggested to my boss that I give up my job, he wouldn't hear of it. The moment he told me I couldn't go, even if I wanted to, that made me want to all the more. We had a real fight about it.' He suddenly smiled, but his smile was not gay. 'And then I guess partly it was just what you might call a naïve, romantic desire to escape, to get away as far as possible from where I happened to be – the feeling that if I could get into a nice, new uniform I'd become a nice, new person. It seemed to me then, in fact it still seems to me –' his voice became hesitant, as if he feared that she might laugh at him –'that there's something peculiarly clean in direct action, and most of all in action that involves a measure of risk.'

'I think I see just how you felt,' she exclaimed, 'though I don't think I'd describe it in the same way. And I never thought of war's being clean, Ralph. Think of the trenches, think of the jungles, think of the smashed men and ships!'

'I'm sure war itself is foul', he said. 'I'm sure it's just as hellish as it was in Sherman's time. Probably more so. I've no doubt I'll hate it. But there are different kinds of hells. I don't think for me, at least, that it will be the worst kind.'

'What other kinds do you mean?' she asked softly, although she felt that she should not.

He gave her another long look, and once more the rest of the people were pushed far away. 'Perhaps one of the worst,' he said slowly, 'is realizing the possible heavens you have missed.'

This time she dropped her glance before his; and then swiftly, with a feeling that she was running away, she told him of her anonymous warning which just now seemed quite unimportant.

But it evidently didn't seem unimportant to Ralph. 'Good God, Kate!' he exclaimed. 'You shouldn't have come!' And then he added: 'Not that I'm not thankful you did.'

'You really think it means something then?' she asked.

'I haven't the faintest idea,' he said, 'but I don't like it. Why on earth should anyone threaten you?'

'June got a warning too', she said. 'I wasn't the only one.'

'Look here,' Ralph exclaimed, 'does anybody else know about this?'

'I told Professor Hatfield about mine', she said. 'That was on the way out here this afternoon. I didn't know then about June's.'

'I'm glad you told him', he said. 'The professor's the only person I trust around here.' And Kate caught herself being surprised at the fact that she was *not* surprised at Ralph's excluding Clotilde from the people whom he trusted. 'I think we ought to tell him about June's letter too. I think he ought to know everything that's going on.'

Kate, strangely, now could feel almost glad that she had been threatened; if Ralph's face showed anxiety, it also showed a new alertness. It was as if a flame which had been smouldering in the tight prison of his inner mind had suddenly been offered an outlet, and now could give not only heat but light.

'I'd love to tell Mr. Hatfield', she exclaimed. 'I like him very much.'

She turned from Ralph toward the professor, and at the same instant he turned toward her, so that she half suspected he might have overheard something of her talk with

Ralph. But if he had, his ears must be extraordinarily sharp.

Mr. Hatfield listened to her attentively, with the dry, ingratiating air which already she had come to know.

'I'm familiar with the cave June described to you', he said. 'Some duck hawks nest in the cliff beneath that particular bluff.'

'But what does it mean, Professor?' Ralph exclaimed. 'The whole thing sounds crazy to me, but you expect things to be crazy around here. Does it mean that Kate – and June – are in any danger?'

'The only thing we know it means,' Professor Hatfield said, 'is that some stranger obviously is, or has been, lurking in the neighbourhood. I think I will investigate that cave, though I suppose by now he will have moved out, that is if he had anything to do with June's letter. Of course we can't positively assume that he did. If he really did, it does seem to make it a rather more elaborate plot, doesn't it?'

'A plot!' Kate exclaimed. 'Then you really think it is a plot?'

'That's just a manner of speaking', he said in his dry voice, which seemed at the same time so impersonal and so intimate. 'If it's a joke, it's a more elaborate joke.'

'If you ask me,' Ralph said, 'it's one hell of a joke! I'd like to get my hands on whoever thought it up.'

'I hardly think it's a joke,' the professor said doubtfully, 'although there are several people around here who have perhaps what might be described as a perverse sense of humour.'

'But what do you think it is then?' Kate asked. 'There must be something behind it. What is it?' She tried to keep her tone calm.

'My dear Kate,' he said, 'you don't mind if I call you Kate? – I only wish I knew. It interests me enormously.'

'But what do you think I ought to do?'

'Hmmm —' He looked abstractedly at the sweet williams in the centre of the table. 'You know, I don't think it would be a bad plan, if you have no objections, to spread the news to the assembled company. Perhaps there have been more letters. What do you think, Ralph?'

'By all means', Ralph said. 'Let's bring it out into the open. Let's clear the air around here, if that's possible.'

The idea startled Kate: it would focus so much attention on herself; and perhaps June would resent her having told Ralph and Mr. Hatfield. 'You really think we ought to?' she asked.

'I don't see that it would do any harm; and it might – it just might – begin to clear things up. Will you give me permission to go ahead?'

'All right', Kate said rather faintly. She dreaded the next moment, and yet if everyone knew, it might, after all, be more comfortable.

The professor tapped on his glass with his knife, as if he were calling a meeting to order. Everybody turned to look at him.

'I've got a rather strange question to ask the company', he announced. He paused for a moment, as if he enjoyed the suspense; then in a matter-of-fact tone he asked: 'Has any one of you within the last few days received an anonymous letter?'

June, directly across the table from Kate, sent her a startled look, and Kate leaned towards her. 'I thought it was wiser to tell him about it', she said. 'I got one too.'

'An anonymous letter!' Mr. Gladstone exclaimed. 'I used to get them occasionally – quite juicy ones. I always thought they were sent by jealous females, or sometimes possibly by husbands with whose wives I had become acquainted. But that was long ago – in my salad days.'

'Perhaps I had better elucidate', Professor Hatfield went

on, and precisely, neatly, as if he were analysing an experiment before a class, he told them about Kate and June.

'But how perfectly thrilling!' Mavis exclaimed, leaning forward with a shudder and staring at the professor. 'You're not just inventing it, are you, you terrible man? You're not going sadist on us?'

No one else spoke, and Kate followed Professor Hatfield's glance as it moved from face to face about the table.

'I take it then', he said, after nearly a minute, 'that none of the rest of you has received one of these – I suppose I should call them warnings.'

'*I* got one!'

Kate jumped, for the voice, loud and harsh, came from almost directly behind her. Then she realized that it was Ruby who had spoken.

Professor Hatfield glanced at her over his shoulder.

'You say you received one too? May I ask what the message was?'

'Just about the same as June's. "Keep your nose out", it said. Something like that. The other night walking in the woods I heard the bushes rustling. I thought it might be Felix back at his old tricks, with some girl from one of the farms. So I charged, but they were too quick for me, whoever they were. To tell you the truth, I thought Felix might have written that letter. But you can take my word for it, Felix would never write a letter to scare away a young girl from here, not if I know Felix!'

'Ruby darling, we wives do have our troubles, don't we?' Mavis exclaimed, flinging back her head and looking archly over her shoulder; but Ruby paid no attention and continued passing the asparagus.

Chapter Four

IT MUST have been an hour after dinner, though Kate had lost all sense of time, that Mavis rose from her chair. She had drunk several glasses of cognac, which had been served with the coffee out here on the terrace, and now she tottered so wildly that she might have fallen if Jo had not sprung to her rescue.

'If you'll excuse me,' she said, 'all this charming company, I think I'll be going to my room. I don't feel quite up to par all of a sudden. In fact, if you ask me, I feel like hell.'

She let her glance wander vaguely around the dim terrace, noticed Kate, and pulled Jo in her direction. Kate rose to say good night, and to her embarrassment, Mavis flung her arms around her neck and kissed her effusively.

'Good night, darling', she cooed, with a suggestion of a hiccup. 'You're lovely, you're just lovely! You remind me of myself when my name was in lights not so many years ago. I can't ask you to come up to my room, because Jo, the foolish boy, would be so jealous, and I wouldn't be leaving you now, but it's this dizziness, this silly dizziness. Every so often the spells come over me, just like that! The semicircular canals, you know. It seems that mine are particularly semi.'

And leaning against Jo, she wavered into the house.

When Jo returned five minutes later, he paused for a moment on the threshold of the long, lighted window and shook himself delicately, like a cat who had just come in out of the rain.

'And now,' he said, 'that our dear Mavis is safely in Ruby's hands, why don't we all adjourn to my studio and

have a little music? I often do not care to play after such
an excellent dinner, but tonight I feel for some reason
inspired.'

Mr. Gladstone was not enthusiastic.

'My dear fellow,' he said, 'I'm sure it will be wonderful,
but Ralph and I had rather counted on a game of chess
before we go to bed, so perhaps you'll excuse us. How
about it, Ralph?'

'By all means, let's play chess', Ralph said with decision
if not with eagerness. Kate could gather that he, too, was
not fond of Jo.

'I'm sure the music will be a treat for the professor and
Kate,' Mr. Gladstone went on, 'and I know Clotilde
always loves to play for you. More and more, Clotilde
darling, isn't that so? More and more you like to play
with José.'

Clotilde laughed lazily and rose from her chair. 'Father
dear,' she said, 'your first expression was more accurate
– play *for* him, not play *with* him. I love to play for any
good musician who will condescend to let me. Perhaps
you wouldn't quite understand.'

Mr. Gladstone shrugged his shoulders. 'Does one ever
understand one's children?' he exclaimed. 'Come along,
Ralph, let's you and I turn to the comparatively simple
problems of chess.'

Clotilde took Jo's arm, and Kate and the professor followed them around the corner of the house, through a
herb garden, wonderfully fragrant in the soft night air,
to the cottage which she had seen from her window.

When Jo turned on the light, the room looked so large
that she realized it must be the only one, and that the
divan covered with an old Navaho blanket must be Jo's
bed. At the other end of the room stood a grand piano,
and above the fireplace hung a stilted yet clinically detailed painting of St. Sebastian bristling with arrows. It

made Kate rather uncomfortable to look at it, and she shifted her chair slightly.

Professor Hatfield had taken a chair close to hers, and June had slumped down on the divan. 'Golly,' she exclaimed, 'I'm tired! You know, Katey, I was so excited about your coming to-day I woke up at four o'clock this morning.'

The first thing Jo played was a Tartini sonata, and after a few bars Kate realized that he was a first-rate violinist. It interested her that his face, so mobile when he talked, became when he played as quiet as a mask. She had to admit, too, that Clotilde knew what she was about: she had a pleasant touch and followed Jo accurately, although in the final allegro she fumbled the passage work.

As soon as he had finished, Jo put his violin on the piano, and wiped his forehead and neck. Clotilde kept her seat on the bench. 'And what about a Mozart?' she asked. 'Let's try the C major, the one we did the other night.'

'I'm afraid that would go better if you hadn't taken that second cognac', Jo said. 'However, we can try.'

Professor Hatfield rose quickly, almost furtively, from his chair. 'If you will excuse me,' he said in a deprecating voice, 'I think I'll slip along. I find the early morning one of the best times for my observations. And also I hope I may track down an owl or two on the way home. That takes longer than you think. It was very nice, Jo, very nice indeed. Thank you ever so much. And Clotilde, you might thank your good father for me. I don't think I'll disturb them at their game. Good night all!'

He slipped noiselessly out into the darkness, and Kate felt that his last glance had been for her.

At the first bars of the sonata she recognized that it was one she had played often with her brother. She sank back in her chair and closed her eyes, to try to recapture the times when they had played it together at Matunuck, but the Mozart did not go so well: Clotilde was stumbling more and more. Kate looked up and saw that Jo was frowning. Suddenly he put down his violin.

'I think,' he said, with an edge to his voice, 'that it's no use to continue. You must excuse me, Kate, I should have liked to play you Mozart, but circumstances beyond my control —'

'You go to hell!' Clotilde exclaimed in a tone that reminded Kate of the way she had spoken to Mavis this afternoon. 'You ought to keep your mind off your audience, Jo. I don't think this one's too damn critical, if you ask me.'

She rose from the piano bench, opened her compact, and started to put on more lipstick.

Kate was so furious that she could feel herself trembling. She stood up quickly. 'If you'd like to play the Mozart,' she said, 'I'd love to accompany you. I've played it with my brother. In fact we've done almost all the Mozart sonatas together.'

Jo's glance was surprised and a little sceptical.

'Splendid', he said. 'Splendid! We'll try again. But Mozart isn't easy, as our beautiful friend here can testify.'

'No?' Kate said, and realized that her voice was imitating Clotilde's. 'I always thought he was.'

She glanced at June to see what she thought of this audacity, and then smiled in spite of herself. Poor June was now sitting on the edge of the divan, her knees wide apart, her hands drooping between them; her jaw looked as if it would sag at any moment and her eyes seemed dead with sleep. She reminded Kate just then of some big homely puppy trying to keep awake as it stared into the fire.

'June darling!' she exclaimed. 'It's too cruel! You must go right to bed. I hadn't noticed how exhausted you were. You don't have to wait for me.'

June blinked and got up. 'I guess I will at that', she said. 'Good night, Katey. It's great you're here.'

'Good night, little June', Jo called. 'Happy dreams!'

But June left the room without paying the least attention either to him or Clotilde.

As Kate sat down at the piano, she had to exert the greatest effort to keep her fingers from shaking, to fight off that helpless soft feeling in your arms and wrists that makes all control impossible. She knew that Clotilde would watch like a hawk for mistakes, for any clumsiness; she knew that Jo, no matter how many fantastic compliments he paid her, would be annoyed if she bungled. But she did know also that she played more musically than Clotilde, that she had a more finished technique; and she had the advantage of having taken only one cocktail before dinner and having refused the brandy.

She watched Jo out of the corner of her eye for his signal; then, incredibly, they had begun.

Clotilde was standing directly behind her, and it seemed to Kate that she could feel her eyes fixed on her back, trying to hypnotize her so that she would fumble or blur or lose her place. She did not dare let her eyes swerve from one measure to the next; but presently she began to find Clotilde's hostility stimulating – or perhaps it was simply Jo's playing. It was never arbitrary, never sentimental: like an expert dancer, he gave her the feeling that she could not help moving with him, pressing forward or retarding slightly as the music demanded. Soon she forgot Clotilde, and hardly thought of her again until the last chords of the finale.

She turned on the piano bench, doing her best not to look triumphant. To her amazement, Clotilde was not there.

Jo grinned. 'She left', he explained. 'She left in the first movement, as soon as she saw that you played so much better than she does.'

Kate glanced around the room. It was as if she had stepped back into a strange lonely place from a beloved region where everything was beautiful and secure. She remembered suddenly that this was Jo's bedroom as well as his studio.

'I must go now', she said. 'I loved the music. You were very good to let me play for you.'

He shook his head, smiling vividly at her. 'It seems a miracle', he exclaimed. 'She's beautiful; she's wise; and then she turns out to be an excellent musician. But I mustn't try to keep you,' he went on, 'because in the first place I know I should be unsuccessful, and in the second place, between ourselves, I think the exquisite Clotilde wouldn't at all mind if the news spread that you had lingered here with me late at night – if it spread, for example, to Ralph's ears. In fact, I rather suspect that was one of the reasons why she left, counting on your innocence and my experience. But Clotilde does not know me entirely. I am more complicated than she thinks and also more simple. I am, after all, a romantic Spaniard. I divide all women into only two classes, the good and the bad. I love both kinds, but my feelings towards them are quite different. And now good night. I won't go with you. It is better not.'

'Good night', Kate said, and hurried out of the cottage. She hardly knew whether to be pleased or angry or amused; she only knew that she had blushed.

She kept on hurrying across the turf, which felt very wet through her thin slippers. The herb garden was more fragrant than ever, but she did not linger there for a moment. When she turned the corner of the house, she saw that there was no one on the terrace, softly flooded by the light from the long window – no one, that is, unless somebody were crouching behind a chair. She nearly ran across the intervening grass, stepped up on to the tiles, and looked into the living-room. The chessboard, with two or three men left on it, was still spread on a little table, but Mr. Gladstone and Ralph had gone; the big room was empty.

For some reason she shrank from walking through it, as if, once she stepped across the threshold, something would close in behind her and she would be trapped. This was absurd: she must get control of her nerves. She turned away and moved to the edge of the terrace. If she could lose herself in the beauty of this summer night, it should be easier for her to sleep afterward.

The sky was swimming with stars and as she gazed down over the garden she could see more and more clearly the pale windings of the paths, the pattern of the flower beds. Through the quiet air she could hear a faint shrill noise: she could not decide whether it was the sound of crickets or frogs. Whatever it was, it must be far away.

*   *   *   *   *

She did not know how long she had stood there, but she had the feeling all at once that it was very late. It made her think of the times, years ago, when she would wake up in the night and wonder where Father and Mother were, and if they would answer her if she called. Then she would hardly dare to open her mouth, not so much because she was afraid they might scold her as because it would be so awful if no one answered her, if Mother and Father perhaps had died in their sleep, or been taken mysteriously away where she could not reach them. And suddenly this whole night seemed like a huge empty room from which she could not escape, from which no one could rescue her no matter how loudly she called.

There came a sharp rustling from the bushes at the edge of the garden, and she put her hand to her lips, as if to keep herself from crying out.

Then she saw a small black and white object scuttling towards her across the slope of turf between the garden and the terrace. With a gasp of relief she recognized Bobbie; this dear little creature was something warm and natural and friendly. The night was itself once more. She was ashamed of her panic.

She stooped down and called softly: 'Bobbie, Bobbie, you dear little thing, come here! I think you ought to be in bed. We both should be in bed, you and I.'

With a shake of her ears, Bobbie ran up to her and dropped on the tiles at Kate's feet something which she had been carrying in her mouth. Kate thought it might be the string doll she had been playing with this afternoon, and bent forward to look at it.

The glow from the window shone vaguely across the terrace. There was something a little queer about Bobbie's prize: as far as Kate could make out, the string, if it was string, looked finer and silkier than she remembered, with an odd effect, in the diminished light, of being itself luminous.

She reached down in curiosity, picked it up, and realized with a chill of repugnance that it was hair, hair that might be either white or of the palest gold. At the same instant she felt something slimy and warm that slipped down into her palm like a small sluggish reptile. She tried to fling the hair from her, but a strand caught in a ring she was wearing, so that for a moment she could not shake it loose. Then the whole sky reeled, and she in deathly sickness was reeling with it; she heard in the distance a scream which she dimly knew had come from her own throat.

What Bobbie had brought in out of the night was a scalp lock, sticky and bleeding, cut or brutally torn from a woman's head.

Chapter Five

IT SEEMED to Kate that the next instant Mr. Gladstone was crouching beside her, lifting her head and shoulders, but as her brain cleared she suspected that she had been lying there on the tiles for more than a minute.

'My dear Kate,' he exclaimed, 'what happened? Did you see a ghost?'

This was the first time in her life she had fainted and Kate was ashamed of herself. 'No', she said, and tried to smile. 'It was only – it was that awful hair. Where is it?'

She drew in a trembling breath and looked to either side of her. The lock had disappeared, though Bobbie sat a few feet away, staring at her with lowered head and ears drooping forward.

'If you'll help me up —' she said. 'I'm afraid I'm still a bit shaky.'

Then as Mr. Gladstone raised her shoulders and she scrambled to her feet, she saw that the scalp lock had been all the time close beside her: when she had fallen, her dress had covered it. The rushing blackness seethed upward again and for a moment she thought she was gone; but this time she was able to control it.

'There!' she said, and pointed. 'There! You see?'

'Good God!' Mr. Gladstone exclaimed. 'Where in hell did that thing come from?'

'It was Bobbie', she said. 'Bobbie brought it in from the bushes – from the woods, I guess, behind the garden.'

Mr. Gladstone stared out into the night, and Kate, very close beside him, followed his gaze. The next moment she clutched his arm, as she noticed something moving along one of the farther paths.

'Who's there?' Mr. Gladstone called sharply.

'It's Paul Hatfield', a familiar voice answered. 'Is any-thing wrong? Didn't I hear someone scream?'

'We've got something pretty to show you', Mr. Glad-stone said. 'Perhaps you know more about it than we do. It was brought in from the woods.'

'You arouse my curiosity', Mr. Hatfield said, and paused a moment to stoop and greet Bobbie who had streaked across the grass and was now jumping about his legs.

'Was Bobbie with you just now?' Mr. Gladstone asked. 'Did you hear or see anything strange?'

'Bobbie was not with me,' Mr. Hatfield said, crossing the grass to the terrace, 'and the only strange thing I heard was a scream. It gave me quite a start. I was on the track of a great horned owl, where the woods begin to rise towards the bluff. What's the exhibit?'

At that moment Ralph stepped up on to the terrace from around the front corner of the house, and a second later Jo appeared around the other corner, from the herb garden.

'Did I imagine it?' Ralph asked. 'Or did some woman scream?'

'My dear Ralph,' Jo said, 'even my imagination could not have invented that scream – much less yours. Why Paul, you back again? And Kate, my dear child, you still up and about? Don't tell me it was you! Why wasn't I here to protect you?'

'Gentlemen,' Mr. Gladstone announced, 'a minute ago, just before you arrived, Paul asked me what the exhibit was. If you'll step over here, I'll be glad to show you what the dog brought in. It rather disturbed Kate, and I can't say that I wonder.'

For a minute the four men stared down at the bloody dishevelled coil in silence, and Kate, turning away, looked off to the black woods beyond the garden, and the veiled luminous spaces of the sky. She saw a bluish star which she recognized as Vega, but even its familiarity could not break through this dark enchantment. The faraway chirping sound once more filled her ears, and she wondered who else might be listening, from out of that thick shadow.

'But that looks like Clotilde's hair!' Ralph exclaimed suddenly. 'It *is* Clotilde's hair!'

There was such a sharp note of anguish in his voice that Kate, to her bitter shame, felt for an instant a pang of disillusionment, which was swept away at once in her sense of horror. Without another word, Ralph turned and strode into the house, and as Kate watched him running the length of the living-room, her horror became filled with pity.

'At any rate, it's obviously meant to give that impression', Professor Hatfield said after the briefest pause.

'What do you mean?' Mr. Gladstone asked sharply. 'What makes you say that?'

'I only mean,' the professor explained, 'that since Clotilde's hair is such a striking colour, it's natural to assume that any lock of the same colour is hers; but Clotilde is not the only woman in the world whose hair is that shade of very pale gold.'

'We'll soon find out', Mr. Gladstone said in a hard, strained voice. 'Kate, perhaps you'll rouse June and Mavis, if Ralph hasn't. And Jo, you might go for Felix and Ruby, and even the Larsons. I think it might be well to get everyone together.'

'An excellent idea', Mr. Hatfield agreed.

Kate ran through the big room, as Ralph had done the minute before. Jo was close behind her. In the lower hall she stopped for him to catch up with her.

'Which is Mavis' room?' she asked him.

'It's the door opposite the head of the stairs', he said. 'Felix and Ruby have two rooms on the ground floor, in the kitchen wing, so unfortunately we must part company – unless you'd like me to escort you. I'd be delighted.'

'No thanks', Kate said, and hurried up the stairs.

Though no hair could be more unlike June's than that awful sticky lock which she still could see in her mind, coiled like some living thing upon the tiles, it seemed to Kate that the nightmare whose presence she had felt that afternoon lurking in these cheerful rooms, saturating the quiet air of this damp green valley, had begun to manifest itself, and now there would be no stopping. June was the first to have been threatened; and in her eagerness to see that June was all right, Kate had forgotten any other fear.

At the top of the stairs she met Ralph. His face looked white and ravaged. 'Clotilde's not in her room', he said. 'She's not in her bathroom. She's evidently not up there.'

'She couldn't be —?' Kate began, and stopped herself just in time.

But Ralph finished her question for her. 'In Jo's room? Very possibly. That's where I'm going. And then I'm going to have a look around the gardens.'

He brushed past her, and she hurried on until she reached June's door. It was locked; it must be locked on the inside, and that struck her as a good sign. Unless someone had climbed in the window – or through the transom.

She rapped violently on the white panelling. 'June,' she called, 'June dear, are you there? Are you all right?'

She listened as she had never listened before, and presently she could hear something – was it a muffled groan?

'June', she repeated. 'June, answer me. Can you let me in?'

'Katey', a sleepy voice called. 'What is it? Is that you, Katey?'

With a rush of relief that almost took away her breath, Kate realized that the first sound she had heard had merely been the mumbling of someone aroused from sleep.

'Open the door', she said. 'I have to see you.'

In a minute the door opened, and June stood before her in white pyjamas, her hair matted over her forehead and into her eyes like a sheep dog's.

'Get on some clothes,' Kate said, 'and go right downstairs. Something has happened. I must rouse your mother.'

'But Katey —'

'You must do it', Kate said urgently. 'I can't stop to explain. But I'm so glad you're all right, June.'

Then impulsively, in her relief, she kissed June's cheek, and hurried back to the main hallway.

The door of Mavis' room was also locked. She rapped for at least a minute before she heard an answer, and then a querulous and sleepy voice called: 'Do stop that awful noise! It's enough to wake the dead!'

'Mrs. Gladstone,' Kate answered, 'I'm sorry to disturb you but something has happened – something pretty dreadful, I'm afraid. You must get up. You must come downstairs.'

'What do you mean?' Mavis replied, and her voice sounded suddenly awake. 'What has happened?'

'We don't know really, but perhaps — It looks as if someone has been murdered.'

'Murdered!' Her voice rose sharply. 'Someone in this house? Who is it?'

'It may not be as bad as that', Kate said. 'We really know nothing yet. You'll be right down, won't you?' And she turned away from the door.

She was thankful to meet June at the top of the stairs, and took her arm as they went down side by side. When they stepped out on to the terrace, a minute later, neither Jo nor Ralph had returned.

'But Clotilde?' Mr. Gladstone asked sharply. 'She wasn't in her room?'

'No, she wasn't in her room', Kate said. 'Ralph's looking for her outside. Mrs. Gladstone is coming down.'

'If Clotilde has been murdered!' Mr. Gladstone exclaimed, and Kate was surprised, considering the way he had spoken of her, at the savagery in his voice.

'Let me remind you,' Mr. Hatfield said, 'that a scalping such as this is a comparatively minor operation. Painful and terrifying, yes, if performed without anæsthetic; perhaps disfiguring, if the skin and flesh torn away encroach upon the forehead; but not dangerous. And I hardly see, if murder were involved, why anyone should bother with such a trifling addition.'

Jo appeared again around the corner of the house, looked for Kate, and came over at once to stand beside her. He was followed on to the terrace by Mr. and Mrs. Larson, both of them in old flannel wrappers. A moment later Felix and Ruby stepped through the living-room window. Ruby had put a shawl and an apron over her nightgown; Felix was in his shirt and trousers, as if he had not been in bed.

'If you'll give me your attention —' Mr. Gladstone began.

He paused, and Kate, following his glance, saw Mavis hurrying towards them through the living-room. Kate felt that she could gauge her curiosity by the speed with which she had appeared: her face was splotched with powder; she had smeared a daub of red on her lips, and her head was wrapped in a green silk scarf so that none of her hair was visible. She was wearing a peach-coloured *négligé* trimmed with fur.

'What is it?' she exclaimed as she stumbled out on to the terrace. 'Kate hinted at all kinds of horrors.'

'If you will give me your attention,' Mr. Gladstone began again, 'I'll tell you why I've sent for you. A little while ago Bobbie deposited this scalp lock on the terrace. She brought it in from the woods behind the garden – at least from that direction. The hair is the colour and texture of Clotilde's. Kate has just told us that Clotilde is not in her room. Ralph is now looking for her.'

Mavis pushed her way between Jo and Felix. 'Let me see it', she ordered. 'It will probably make me sick, but I must see it. Where —?'

She bent down as she noticed that the lock lay on the tiles in front of her. She glanced dramatically around her, and Kate could picture her raising her finger to her lips; then pulling her *négligé* closely about her she leaned forward as if she were fascinated.

'Yes, that is Clotilde's hair', she said in a half-whisper.

'You're sure?' Mr. Gladstone asked curtly.

Mavis stood up. 'Of course I'm sure', she said in her natural voice. 'It had begun to darken a few years ago and Clotilde had to have it treated every so often. I remember telling her only last week that the muddy natural tint was quite noticeable close to the scalp, and if you examine this, you'll see that I was right. You can tell the difference even out here.'

Mr. Gladstone took a step towards her. 'You hated Clotilde', he said threateningly.

'Yes, I did! I did!' she exclaimed in a rising voice. 'Clotilde deserved anything, but you couldn't think that I — All this is too horrible. It's just come over me. It's really amusing it's so horrible!'

She threw back her head and began to laugh, drawing in her breath like a child with the whooping cough.

Mr. Gladstone gave her a hard slap on the cheek. Mavis shook her head and suddenly became silent.

'I'm sorry, my dear Mavis,' he said, 'but just now Clotilde, although absent, is the centre of the stage.'

'May I suggest,' Felix said, breaking a moment's startled pause, 'that it might be a good thing for someone to call the police. Or perhaps you've already done it, Mr. Gladstone.'

'No, I haven't', Mr. Gladstone said. 'I will.' And he strode into the house.

Vega was still coldly shining in the depths of the summer sky. The air was faintly sweet, not so much, it seemed, from the flowers in the garden, as from the miles and miles of damp sleeping forest. As they stood here now on this dim terrace, waiting for Mr. Gladstone's return, Kate thought all at once of the house before dinner, and the noise, the gaiety as they drank their cocktails; it reminded her of the second act of *Parsifal* when the magic garden is turned into a desert, except that here the spell was not broken; it had only grown darker and more ominous.

In a couple of minutes Mr. Gladstone returned, and with him came Ralph.

'Ralph has been looking everywhere', Mr. Gladstone said grimly. 'He couldn't find a trace of Clotilde. And the telephone's dead. I guess the wire has been cut.'

'But that would mean someone has been up here near the house, wouldn't it?' Jo asked.

'Not necessarily. The wire is brought in from the road on half a dozen trees. Some of them have plenty of branches. You wouldn't even have to climb a pole to cut it.'

'I always said we should have it put underground', Mavis remarked.

'Shut up!' Mr. Gladstone said savagely. Then turning to Felix, he went on: 'Where's the nearest telephone? It would be at the Torgersons', wouldn't it?'

'If you would wait just a minute,' Professor Hatfield suggested before Felix had a chance to reply, 'an idea has occurred to me. It might possibly be well to wait a moment before summoning the police. They are easier to get hold of than to get rid of.'

'But surely —' Ralph began.

'Hear what the professor has to say', Mr. Gladstone ordered. 'What is it, Paul?'

'My idea is this', Professor Hatfield said. 'You can take it for what it's worth. In the first place, this crime, whatever it turns out to be —'

'Whatever it turns out to be!' Mavis exclaimed. 'It's obviously murder. Clotilde's murder.'

'Will you shut up?' Mr. Gladstone rumbled, and Kate could imagine him striking her again.

Professor Hatfield cleared his throat. 'I was going to say that the performance of the crime must have been upset by Bobbie's getting hold of the lock. All of us who know Bobbie realize that no one could count upon her neatly delivering it here – even if it were someone whom she knew well. With due respect to her owners, Bobbie cannot be described as a well-disciplined dog.'

'Are you implying,' Jo asked, 'that this thing was done by someone whom Bobbie knew, some one of us?'

'I'll request nobody to interrupt the professor for any reason whatever', Mr. Gladstone said fiercely. 'Now, Paul —'

'It might be well to state first,' Mr. Hatfield went on, 'that I'm implying nothing. I'm merely trying to explain what seems to me to have happened, on the basis of the facts we know. I think, then, we can take it that the schedule of the crime must have been upset by Bobbie's action. Undoubtedly the scalping was an important part of the crime. In fact, as far as we know, it may be the whole crime.'

Kate noticed that Mavis was about to interrupt again, caught her husband's eye, and subsided with a shrug of her shoulders. As the professor continued talking, in his dry meticulous voice, Kate felt that she was attending a strange class in a nightmare. She glanced at the faces she could see; every one was concentrating upon his words; she could imagine a shadowy blackboard behind him; each sentence seemed clear and reasonable, and yet the whole thing, like the phrases in a dream when you try to remember them later, was fantastic.

'When I say "the whole crime",' he went on, 'I'm simply suggesting that we haven't the faintest proof Clotilde has been murdered. The criminal, however, we do know, cut the telephone wires. That was an added detail, an added risk. He must have realized that we could use another telephone, that we could reach one in a very few minutes. Since the police could not get here in less than half an hour, those few extra minutes couldn't make much difference to him. Why then did he go to the trouble of cutting the telephone wire? He must have felt, it seems to me, that if he could postpone our telephoning for only a few minutes, he might be able to persuade us not to telephone at all. He could only do that by providing us with some reason in consideration of which we ourselves might decide we did not want to telephone – in other words, some reason why we should prefer not to notify the police. If the crime had been allowed to take what I might describe as its due course – a course which we can now trace back as far as June's mysterious letter of nearly a week ago – I suspect we should have received some word, some warning to that effect, not later than our discovery of the crime itself. That was all I wished to say.'

'In other words,' Ralph remarked in a dry unnatural voice, 'you're telling us you think the criminal is trying to do precisely what you yourself are doing at this moment: stalling us off from the police.'

Professor Hatfield looked pleased, Kate thought; in fact he almost seemed to smile.

'Very neatly put', he said. 'Very exact. I suppose I may be acting as a kind of providential proxy for the criminal. But if so, I'm acting not only in his interests but in our own as well. But I could hardly expect my tactics, however ingenious, to keep you from telephoning very long, unless something should occur to substantiate my hypothesis. In the meanwhile, since various ones of us, including yourself, I believe, Ralph, were out of doors at the time, it might be well if we'd each say exactly where we were and what we were doing. Who knows? One of us may unwittingly have seen some trace of the criminal or observed some clue. I'll begin with myself. I was in the woods, near the foot of the bluff. I was looking for an owl I'd observed there only last night. Although I was in somewhat the same direction, apparently, from which Bobbie appeared, I heard nothing out of the way or unusual until Kate's scream. I then came here with all possible haste. And now —' He turned to Mr. Gladstone, as if he were introducing the next speaker at a banquet – 'perhaps you will question the rest of us, Norman. It will be simpler to have some kind of orderly procedure.'

'I agree with you', Mr. Gladstone said. 'I might say that I was in my study looking up some chess problems. When I heard Kate's scream, I came out here at once. Ralph and I had stopped our game a good half hour before. You said you were going for a walk, Ralph. Where did you go and what did you see?'

'I walked down to the main road, and then up to the top of the hill in the direction of town', Ralph said stiffly. 'I heard an owl. I heard a whippoorwill. I saw a rabbit or two. That was all. Not a sign of a human being. No cars passed me. I was a hundred feet or so outside the gate when I thought I heard a scream.' He paused, and for that instant Kate felt that he was shuddering. 'I wasn't sure where it came from,' he went on directly, 'but I thought it was from the house.'

Mr. Gladstone glanced around as if to decide whom he would question next. 'And you, Olaf,' he asked, 'where were you?'

'I was asleep in my bed', Mr. Larson told him, with his

Norwegian accent. 'Emmy and I were both asleep. We were sleeping since nine until he came to wake us up.'

'You couldn't have seen much then', Mr. Gladstone said, and Kate noticed that when he spoke to Olaf his tone was kinder than she had yet heard it. 'What about you, Felix?'

'I was doing a crossword puzzle in my room', Felix said. 'I may have heard the scream, but of course that's on the other side of the house, and it was so faint I didn't pay any attention. When I'm doing those puzzles, I'm just about lost to the world.'

'And Ruby?'

'I was in my bed and asleep', Ruby said shortly.

'What about you, Jo?'

'Like several other of you gentlemen,' Jo said, 'I was taking a stroll. I had been playing. My emotions were a little disturbed.' He paused, and Kate looked away as he sent her a meaningful glance. 'I thought a walk on this lovely night would prepare me for sleep. I too heard the scream. I know so little of your night animals, I thought it might be one of them. Then I said to myself: "That scream is horribly human. It is the scream not of an injured body but of a terrified soul. I'd better investigate", so I turned back and found you here on the terrace.'

Kate started, as someone behind seized her arm. Looking around, she saw June who was staring across the garden, in the direction from which Bobbie had come.

'Kate,' she whispered, 'did you see anything move over there?'

'Where?' Kate asked. 'In the garden?'

'Yes – yes! I saw it too!' It was Mavis' voice, with again a tinge of hysteria in its rising inflection. She had pushed in between Kate and Jo and stood in complete silence since Mr. Gladstone had spoken to her so fiercely. 'Something dark and swooping!'

'Did you really see anything, Mavis?' Mr. Gladstone asked sternly. 'If so, tell us what it was.'

'I don't know', Mavis faltered. 'I couldn't describe it. It was something that moved stealthily, over there, near the end of the garden, beyond the sundial.'

Kate herself, as she peered into the shadows, could see no trace of movement anywhere; then she could imagine that the whole darkness was seething like live steam.

'It will do us no good inventing things', Mr. Gladstone growled. 'There's enough that's real, without that.'

But at that moment Bobbie ran barking down the grassy slope, not towards the sundial where everyone had been looking, but to the nearer edge of the garden, at the left, where one of the paths skirted some lilac bushes.

'What's that she's got?' Mr. Gladstone called. 'Take it from her! Hurry!'

And Kate, with a dizzy feeling, saw Bobbie, not ten yards away standing over some small white object, giving little playful growls and grunts, as if she would defend it with her life.

Ralph stooped, brushed Bobbie aside, and picked it up. 'It's a letter!' he exclaimed. 'At least I think it is. It's an envelope and it's weighted – I suppose so he could shy it further.' He handed it to Mr. Gladstone. 'Jo! Felix!' He shouted with a kind of fierce exuberance. 'Come along! Let's see if we can catch him!'

The next instant the three men had dashed across the garden and were plunging into the woods, with Bobbie yodelling at their heels.

'What is it?' Mavis asked eagerly of Mr. Gladstone, as he stepped back on to the terrace. 'Who's it from? What does it say?'

'That I shall know presently, when I have read it', Mr. Gladstone answered her curtly, and slipped the letter into his pocket.

'Olaf,' he said, 'I see no reason why you and Emmy shouldn't go back to bed. And you too, Ruby.'

'Good night, sir', Olaf said, and he and his wife walked around the corner of the house into the darkness. Ruby, without a word, tramped back through the living-room.

Mr. Gladstone drew out a large pocket handkerchief, spread it by its two upper corners, as if he were a magician about to perform a trick. Then he stooped, put it over the bloody lock, wrapped the linen carefully around it, picked up the small bundle, and followed Ruby into the house.

Kate caught herself guessing what he would do with it. Would he put it in a safe? In the icebox? In a bureau drawer? What would you do with your daughter's scalp? A question for Emily Post.

The lock, she noticed, had left a smear on the tiles, like the trace of some gigantic slug. She drew in her breath sharply. It required all the strength of her will not to start laughing hysterically, as Mavis had done; and once she had started, she felt that she could never stop.

Fortunately at that moment June put her arm around her and held her tight. 'It's not fair!' she exclaimed in an intense passionate voice which brought Kate at once to herself. 'I got you into this, Katey. It's all my fault. I brought you out here. You must go away tomorrow. I can't keep you here now. Clotilde didn't even get one of those letters, and look what they did to her!'

'I'm in no danger', Kate said. 'No one's after me. How do you think I'd feel if I ran away?'

June's arm tightened about her with an almost savage energy.

'I want you to go!' she exclaimed. 'I couldn't bear it if anything happened to *you*.'

'You can't get rid of me as easily as that', Kate said, but she felt that her tone was shamefully fainthearted.

Chapter Six

'I F YOU'D only tell us what's in the envelope', Mavis urged. 'Norman, you're positively sadistic, keeping us in suspense like this.'

'I told you once,' Mr. Gladstone said coldly, 'that when Jo and Felix and Ralph come back, you shall hear all about it – not that I think it will give you much pleasure. In the meanwhile I'm in no mood for obscene female curiosity.'

They had been sitting here in the living-room, Kate supposed, for not more than twenty-five minutes, but she had the impression that there were infinite wastes of night behind her, all around her. On the drowsy fringes of her memory were hours when, as a child, she had waited in dentists' offices, waited so long, it seemed, that her fear had been drained of its living quality and simply lay on her mind like something inert and dead, an indistinguishable part of the boredom of prolonged suspense. Mr. Gladstone sat in a big chair near the fireplace, and the lamp on the table beside him emphasized the pockets beneath his eyes, the sagging of his jowls; as he glowered at the empty hearth, it seemed to Kate that he had aged in the course of the evening. Mavis, slumped in the chair opposite his, kept yawning nervously; her powder had settled into the wrinkles of her cheeks and gave her face a scaly appearance suggestive of leprosy. Kate was glad that at least June was beside her here on the sofa. At first they had talked to each other in low voices, but now June's face had stiffened into a sleepy mask. Only Professor Hatfield seemed to be content with the situation: he had picked up a copy of *Time* magazine and was reading with every sign of interest, his head cocked to one side.

Kate hardly noticed it when at last Bobbie walked in from the terrace, her tongue lolling out, her head drooping so that her ears almost swept the floor. But the next minute Ralph and Felix entered, with Jo a few steps behind them. Their damp shirts clung to their bodies; a twig was still caught in Ralph's hair.

Mr. Gladstone raised his head without otherwise changing his position, and stared sombrely at them. He reminded Kate just then of a corrupt and powerful Renaissance pope receiving a legation.

'Well?' he asked.

The three men glanced at each other. Then Felix spoke.

'I'm sorry, sir,' he said, 'but we didn't find a sign of anyone or anything. I went up to the left, to the top of the bluff through the woods, and Bobbie was with me. She carried on so at first, I thought we might be on the trail of someone. Then she left me and joined Mr. Ralph who was working along through the bottom lands. Mr. Jo says he went down towards the road and the open fields. Coming back, not five minutes ago, I thought I had some one sure, but it was only Mr. Jo and Mr. Ralph.'

The smooth respect with which he spoke to his employer did not prevent, Kate thought, a tinge of irony in the 'Mr.'s' that he attached to the names of Ralph and Jo.

'It occurred to me,' Ralph said, 'that it would be easy to get down the bluff to the river. If there was a small boat ready, a man, or a group of men, could be miles downstream by now. Or they could land on the other side. With the bluffs and the bottom lands going on for miles, a gang might stay hidden indefinitely.'

'You seem to have given some study to the terrain', Mr. Gladstone said dryly. 'But now I should like to read you the interesting letter that was thrown into the garden. It is printed in red crayon which, Professor Hatfield tells me, seems to be quite a fetish of our correspondent – that is, if one assumes that all the letters were sent from the same source.'

He spread open the folded sheets of paper, looked around at his audience for a moment, and began reading as if the message were of no personal concern to himself or anyone present.

My dear Mr. Gladstone:

In spite of the rather sensational way in which this has reached you, it is merely a routine business letter. My friends and I should like you to hand over fifty thousand dollars. Since we prefer it in cold cash, in bills no larger than $50, and since naturally you do not have that much on hand, we will give you until day after tomorrow, which allows you the whole of tomorrow to make arrangements. In day after tomorrow's (Saturday's) mail you will receive instructions as to where and when we should like it delivered. As you see, this is just the old kidnapping racket.

If there is any new twist to it, it is because we have noticed that kidnapping in the past has often failed because the kidnappers had either too little imagination or too much sentiment. They haven't put themselves in the place of the victim's family. Their threats have been unconvincing, and sometimes they have failed to carry them out.

I can understand the temptation on your part to call in the police. 'How will the kidnappers know?' you say to yourself. 'We'll take a chance on it.' Mr. Gladstone, you may take a chance, but it is to convince you of the imprudence of such a course that we are sending you the scalp of your daughter, Clotilde. If we have the slightest reason to suspect that this affair is mentioned to the police, or to any living soul outside this immediate household, you will receive other, and more essential portions of your daughter's very lovely body, chosen in such a way that she may, by the grace of God, still survive.

You will be relieved to hear, I know, that the little operation does not seem to have affected her general health, but I'm sorry to say that her morale is definitely low. She's the type of girl who believes in taking chances, I guess, but I'm sure she would join me in urging you not to take this one.

Our real talking point, however, is not only what may happen to Clotilde. I say this so you won't feel inclined, at any time, to write her off as a total loss. When it comes to prying loose a sum of money, even such a trifle as $50,000, we believe the more leverage the better. So we're not just counting on the little surgical operations you might force us to perform on Clotilde, but on what will happen to June as well, if the cash isn't delivered without any monkey business. We are using Clotilde as a kind of sample or warning.

I must tell you that if any attempt is made to smuggle June out of this region, as a protective measure, we will finish off Clotilde in some appropriate manner, and also some of the boys would then count on having a little fun with her first. Also, I can promise you that sooner or later we'd catch up with the unlucky June.

For every reason then we suggest that you will comply with our demand. We know it is well within your means. We have taken care to be reasonable. Even a father's heart might hesitate to part with, say, $200,000. One sign of the lack of imagination in kidnappers is their

failure to understand how much even the very wealthy
– or I might say, most of all the very wealthy – hate to
part with large sums of money. But $50,000 – that is a
small affair. We don't insult you by suspecting that you
will hesitate. Come across, and everything will be all
right except the little matter of Clotilde's scalp, and
damage there can be hidden by the right kind of hair-
do. Hold back, gossip with a neighbour, call in the
police, and you, and your two daughters, I do assure
you, will be sorry.

At the mention of her name June had clutched Kate's
fingers, and now in the moment of silence as Mr. Gladstone's voice stopped abruptly, Kate thought that she
could hear June's heart thumping; or perhaps it was her
own that she heard. The long bright room, the group of
people, surrounded her like a wavering film that barely
managed to keep out an abyss of darkness; the only real
thing was the feeling of June's palm pressed tightly against
hers, the hot grip of her fingers. For June's sake, for the
sake of this child who trusted her, whose sole friend she
was, she must keep her head. In this horrible time she
must prove herself of some use.

'Perhaps you can guess my reason for reading you this
literary effort', Mr. Gladstone continued grimly. 'Among
other things it's a proof of the intelligence of Professor
Hatfield, to whom I'm deeply grateful.' He gave a sharp
glance from the corner of his eye at the professor. 'I should
certainly curse myself if I had got in touch with the police.
And now I make to you all the absolute request that none
of you, for any reason whatever, say a word to a living
soul of what has happened. It may be just as well that
the telephone is disconnected; though on second thoughts,
perhaps not. You'd better get in touch with the company
tomorrow, Felix, unless you find that you can fix the wire.

6

It's conceivable that the kidnappers might want to call us up. As they state in their letter, their demand under the circumstances is moderate. I believe in taking chances for myself, but not for my daughters. If any of you, deliberately or accidentally, should spread any hint of the state of affairs, I'll hold him completely responsible for the results. And now, good night, everybody!'

He slouched heavily to the door; then, looking back, he added with a suggestion of his sardonic smile:

'I'm afraid it would be useless to wish you pleasant dreams.'

Chapter Seven

As she stood in the sun, the next morning, on the grassy bank that skirted the front of the house, Kate felt it was lucky perhaps that she could not remember her dreams.

Mavis had not appeared for breakfast, and every now and then Kate had caught herself thinking of Clotilde, also, as lying comfortably in bed. This would remind her, each time with a new shock, of the unspeakable reality, and for a moment she could not force herself to eat. Ralph had greeted her with a fixed smile which made her think of the way he had looked at Clotilde yesterday on the terrace. For that *was* yesterday, of course: to-day was only Friday, though she could hardly make herself realize it. In spite of herself she could not keep a shade of reproach from her own glance as she returned his 'Good morning'. Certainly she had done nothing to make him feel that for her he must put on a mask. Then his smile had wavered. The mask was still there; but it was as if, through the painted cloth grown slightly transparent, she had caught a glimpse of distorted tense muscles, but so obscure a glimpse that she could not interpret their expression: it might be anguish, or shame – or terror. He had eaten hurriedly and excused himself before the rest. Even Jo had hardly spoken; but Mr. Gladstone had made a number of carefully trivial remarks; it was clear he intended that, so far as possible, life at the farm should proceed as usual to-day.

'June,' he said after breakfast, 'be sure you're back from your ride by half past ten. Felix is going with you. He's driving me into town at eleven, to the bank, and if you're late I'll give you hell.'

When June had said she did not want to ride, he had flared up.

'You're going as usual', he said harshly. 'Damn you, don't you see that if you once give in to this infernal business, you're lost!'

June had merely scowled at him; then she had turned without a word and gone upstairs. Kate had followed her to her room.

'He's right, June', she said, as June was changing into her riding clothes. 'We mustn't give in.' But June had remained sullen.

'It's all very fine for you to talk', she exclaimed. 'He's not your father, the damn fool!' And Kate had made a pretence of laughing, as if it were a joke.

Now as she watched June and Felix, both very spruce and correct on their bay horses, trotting down the driveway, with Bobbie scampering beside them, she wondered what she should do for the next hour. June had promised that she would teach her to ride, but Kate was just as glad the lesson had not started this morning. The only person she could bear to see at present was Ralph; she felt that he would want to be left alone; so she avoided the house and walked around over the lawn to the garden.

As the sun glistened on the pink gravel paths, the turf edgings, burning up the dew that remained on the leaves and petals, it was hard to associate this spot with the shadowy terror of last night. A catbird alighted on the sundial and stared at her. The top of its grey back, the surface of each leaf, the spaces of lawn, the loop of the distant road, were all reflecting in their separate colours the shimmering blue sky. 'I mustn't give in!' she repeated to herself. 'I mustn't give in! I must take each hour as it comes and not let myself start imagining.'

Nonetheless, when someone called her name from behind the hedge of junipers that separated the garden from the woods, she barely checked her impulse to cry out, before she recognized the voice as Professor Hatfield's.

'Kate', he called softly. 'Listen to me, my dear. I'm sorry if I startled you. I've been in the offing for the last hour or so, hoping I could make contact with you. Walk to the arch that leads out of here. I've got several things I'd like to say to you.'

Puzzled and a little annoyed with him for the scare he had given her, Kate followed the path to the rose-covered archway that led into the woods. As she stepped through it, out of the glare of the garden into the damp shadow, it was like walking into a vault. Professor Hatfield was waiting for her, standing with what struck her as almost unnatural stillness at the foot of a hickory tree.

'I don't see why you had to be so mysterious, even if you did want to speak to me', she said irritably. 'What difference would it make if anyone saw us?'

'My dear girl, I can quite understand', he said in a soothing tone. 'Naturally it's disconcerting to have your name called from out of a bush, especially after what happened last night. And very possibly there's no earthly reason why everyone in the house shouldn't know of our meeting this morning, but I would rather err on the safe side. Perhaps you can guess why I want to talk to you.'

'I'm afraid I can't', she said, still a little coldly.

'Well,' he said, as if eager to be quite fair, 'that's natural too. As a matter of fact, there are really several different reasons – different though interrelated. In the first place, I felt I ought to caution you.'

'Caution me', she repeated, in uneasy surprise. 'Against what?'

His thin lips smiled at her. 'Well, let's say against coming out into the dark woods, when somebody calls your name mysteriously from behind a tree, as I did just now. Especially if there is no one else around.'

Her heartbeats quickened unpleasantly. As she looked at him, here in this deep-green shadow, standing with such almost furtive stillness under the tree, she could imagine that his unblinking eyes which had yesterday reminded her of a bird's were instead the eyes of a snake.

'Don't be silly!' she exclaimed with somewhat forced impatience. 'Didn't you want to come?'

'Yes, my dear Kate, I did,' he said, 'and I assure you I'm quite harmless. But perhaps someone else would not have been.'

'I'd probably have run for the house,' she said, 'if I hadn't recognized your voice.'

'Ah, but that's the point I'm trying to make', he exclaimed. 'Just because you recognize the voice of someone doesn't necessarily mean that he's not dangerous.'

Again, for a moment, her heart felt too big for her chest; it took an effort to breathe naturally. 'You mean that someone I know – someone in the house – may be dangerous? You mean that someone in the house may be connected – with this – with Clotilde?'

'That's precisely what I mean,' he said with a confidential drop in his voice, 'and that's why I thought it might be just as well if no one saw that you and I were having this little talk. He might have suspected that we were up to something. It might have put him on his guard.'

'But who is he?' she asked incredulously. 'How can you know?'

'I don't know', Professor Hatfield admitted. 'And even if I knew that it was some member of the household, I wouldn't have the slightest idea who. That's another reason why I wanted to see you. You are completely an outsider. It's obvious that you at least could have nothing to do with this. It would have been ironic should I have chosen the criminal to confer with. So I thought that you were the logical person to help me discover if possible who he is.'

She shrank from this idea as if he had offered her some poisonous thing to eat.

'But it can't be anyone in the house,' she exclaimed the next moment in relief, 'because everyone was gathered on the terrace when that dreadful letter was thrown into the garden.'

'Ah but,' he said, 'to abduct a young woman and hold her somewhere for ransom would obviously require more than one person. Two people, I should say, at the very least, when you consider the necessity for first-aid treatment. I'm merely suggesting that one of them, and it seems to me highly probable the guiding mind of the scheme, belongs to the household.'

They had been walking slowly along a path through the woods and now they came to a small six-sided summer-house of mossy latticework. A Virginia creeper covered one side of it and had reached from the top to the overhanging branch of an oak tree.

'We might go in and sit down', he suggested. 'The chairs are comfortable and you look as if you had found the strain of the last twelve hours a little wearing.'

He stood back courteously for Kate to enter first. The light in here was even dimmer and greener than outside; only a few intensely white spots of sun, piercing the leaves and the latticework, brought out as in a detailed drawing the grain of the old wooden floor and made the prevailing shadow deeper and more liquid. Once again Kate had the sense that this whole valley, like a lost region in a fairy tale, was buried under deep water – water that little by little would chill you to the bone and prevent your breathing.

'But why should it be someone in the house?' she asked with an effort, after she had seated herself in a low wicker arm-chair. 'It's horrible, it's ridiculous, to think that someone here on the farm would do such a thing.'

'Horrible, I admit', he said. 'Ridiculous, no. Let me give you some of my reasons. How many people outside this household, do you think, knew that you were coming here to the farm? I'm the only friend the family sees much of out here, and Mr. Gladstone hadn't even mentioned it to me. I doubt if anyone knew, unless he were purposely informed of the fact. The farm keeps very much to itself nowadays; it's a little community of its own, as I told you yesterday; and yet you received that warning letter. You can see that if there was any scheme involving June, a loyal friend who might be expected to be with her most of the time would be a major complication, but nonetheless that note was a mistake. If I had been arranging things, I never would have allowed it to be sent. And then there's the question of Bobbie. We know she must have been somewhere near when the abduction, and the mutilation, occurred. Had there been only strangers she would undoubtedly have barked, or rather howled, with that particularly piercing voice she has begun to develop; and even if it had been as far away as the main road we would have heard her. Whereas she would have slipped along after one of the household without making a sound. Then consider the actual technique of the crime. Clotilde was probably approached fairly near the house by someone who on one pretext or another lured her further away. It would be far simpler if this were someone she knew and felt completely at home with. It seems probable that she was engaged in conversation when an accomplice attacked her from behind, and knocked her unconscious or possibly drugged her. It seems almost certain, moreover, that whoever managed the affair was thoroughly familiar with the ways of the household. After all, there are a great many people around here.'

'You needn't go on', Kate said. 'I can see your point. But Professor Hatfield, why should they do such a thing? It wouldn't be just for that money, would it – especially if they had to divide it up?'

'I hate to think,' he said, 'how many crimes have been committed – brutal, hideous crimes – for far smaller sums. Various people in our little group, to start with myself, could gladly do with more cash. There's Felix, Jo, Ralph, Mavis —'

'Mavis —' Kate exclaimed. 'You surely don't think that Mavis —'

'I'm only saying that Mavis, along with the others, could gladly do with fifty thousand, or even a share of it. Most of Mr. Gladstone's money came from his first wife, Clotilde's mother. Mavis didn't have a thing. She has to get along on what Norman gives her and she doesn't like it. But I think you're quite right in this case not to consider merely the money motive. I shouldn't be at all surprised if a good part of it were budgeted as wages for the outside help, whose responsibility and risk it will be to collect it. Though of course there may be a second demand, after the first is acceded to. It would be a piquant touch, for example, to ask for another fifty thousand for medical expenses.'

'But then, if it's not the money,' Kate asked wearily, 'what other motive —?'

Professor Hatfield gave his dry chuckle. 'I said not *merely* the money', he corrected. 'Undoubtedly it entered into the scheme. But my dear girl, there is a whole tangle of plausible personal motives to back it up. Let's start with Mavis: as you no doubt have guessed she couldn't abide Clotilde. Clotilde has always resented her father's second marriage, and lately there has been the question of Jo. Jo belonged to Mavis. Mr. Gladstone who is not old-fashioned and who is perhaps a shade cynical did not object to the situation, and I think it rather amused him. But when Clotilde came back from New York this spring, Jo began to find her very attractive – much more so, I'm afraid, than poor old Mavis. Jo loves comfort but he also loves beauty. However, Clotilde was engaged to Ralph. She'd met him last winter in New York where he was working in the Bell Laboratories, waiting for his navy commission to come through. Apparently she took him by storm. Clotilde, to speak mildly, is a rather domineering, a rather spoiled girl, but she can be as smooth as silk when she wants to. She is used to getting whatever she sets her heart on. As Ralph came to know her better, to see her in her native habitat, he began to regret the situation – unless I've read the signs all wrong. All the more so, as Clotilde seemed to find Jo intensely congenial. Personally, I think she was only trying to hold Ralph by stirring up his jealousy. Now Jo is clever – more so than you might think; he's also fiery. It wouldn't be surprising if he realized that Clotilde was using him for a purpose, and *that* he would certainly resent. Clotilde, I regret to say, rather enjoys leading men on. Even Felix. Clotilde, at one time, deliberately played up to him in a fashion that almost suggested the Countess Julie, if you're familiar with the plays of Strindberg. It wouldn't be surprising if Felix detested her, and I know Ruby does. So you see . . .'

'Yes, I see', Kate said, and rose from her chair: she felt she had heard about as much as she could stand, and perhaps the worst thing of all was having Ralph involved. As she thought of his face at breakfast, it seemed, incredibly, as if he too might have been bewitched by the foul enchantment of this place. 'But it sounds so fantastic!' she broke out. 'Suppose everything is like that, you still can't make me believe that any of these people would do such a – such a ghastly thing, for any of those reasons.'

Professor Hatfield got up also. 'I quite agree with you',

he exclaimed. 'I said the motives were plausible: they are
merely that, if one is considering normal individuals. I
don't think any of those motives, even with the money
added, would be enough in itself to account for this particular crime. It has an atmosphere of its own, a kind of
gratuitous ferocity, of macabre though quite unoriginal
fantasy, that points to a very special type of mind in the
person who conceived it.'

'You mean,' she asked, 'that you think he's mad?'

'It depends on what you mean by mad', he said. 'In the
usual sense, no. We had a case here in Woodside last
summer of a man who really was insane, obsessed by a lust
for killing; I had something to do with it myself – in fact,
I had the honour to figure for a time as a suspect' – he
gave his little chuckle – 'and this, I think is quite different.
The lust killer, apart from his obsession, may be a sensitive
and scrupulous man; his particular urge is too much for
him, that's all. But the thing that marks our present man
is his complete absence of scruple. He must be someone for
whom the moral world, the world of kindly human emotions, of love, of pity, of altruism, simply does not exist, except perhaps as an intellectual abstraction. In other words,
he must be what is sometimes called a moral imbecile.'

'But I thought an imbecile,' Kate said, 'was the same as
a feeble-minded person, only even less developed.'

'Not a moral imbecile', he explained. 'Such people are
not infrequently intelligent and quite normal except that
they have no sense of right or wrong. If they tortured an
animal, it would not be so much through sadism, which
implies a measure of sympathy, even if perverted, as
through idle curiosity. They might choke a baby to death,
if its crying annoyed them. They might wreck a whole
trainload of people, if it seemed a safe way to kill off a
creditor among them.'

Kate shuddered and stepped out of the summerhouse

on to the shaded path. Professor Hatfield's description seemed to her particularly chilling and revolting. It suggested a human being who was yet not human, a stranger, an outcast who lived in the midst of men and yet inhabited a cold, dreadful world of his own. Then, across the years, she remembered once when she was a little girl standing with Mother in the Jardin des Plantes in Paris and watching the hyenas. Their hair was so rubbed off, so scanty, that she could see patches of pale pinkish skin on their tight bodies. It looked almost like coarse human skin, and suddenly she had seen them not as animals but as monstrous deformed people; she could imagine them rising on their hind legs and walking towards her, with their flat heads thrust forward, their mouths dripping; she could imagine them trying to talk to her, to call her by name; and the idea had terrified her so that she began to scream, and she could never bear to tell Mother why. This man seemed such a creature as they. And according to Professor Hatfield, she might be living under the same roof with him; she might have talked with him, have shaken his hand; to-day she might be seeing him again. For an instant she could almost smell a faint animal stench. The white spots of sunlight stabbing through the leaves danced before her eyes. She swallowed mechanically; and then she realized that she must look ill, for Professor Hatfield had taken her arm and was guiding her gently along the path.

'Perhaps you see now why I spoke to you', he said. 'Such a man – such a mind – is dangerous; once he has begun a career of actual violence he rarely stops. You and June, who have received letters, have already attracted his attention. Frankly, nothing would relieve me more than to know he was safely behind bars.'

'But what can I do?' Kate asked, and her voice sounded to herself far away.

'You can keep your eyes and ears open. You can notice

anything unusual, even if it seems to you quite insignificant, and you can report it to me. But I see that you don't feel well. Perhaps it is too much to ask. Perhaps I should advise you to leave at once, to go home. In fact, my dear Kate, I'll drive you into town myself this afternoon, if you don't think you can bear it out here.'

The possibility of escape dazzled her; it was as if she had been shot to the surface of the water, had filled her lungs with clean fresh air. But this lasted only for an instant: there was the question of June. She had come out here, really, to help June, and now the poor girl needed her a hundred times more than ever. If Ralph were not here, Kate felt, perhaps she could not have borne it, but with Ralph to rely on, strange and tortured though he seemed, there would be no excuse for running away.

'I'll stay!' she burst out passionately, half resentfully. 'Of course I can't go now. It would be mean for me to go!'

'I admire your decision', he said, and gave her arm a friendly squeeze. 'And you can think of this, my dear. If anything we unearth results in rescuing Clotilde a day, or even an hour sooner, it may save her life or her reason. Clotilde is not an entirely sympathetic character; but I've always felt sorry for her. Such an upbringing as hers is not calculated to foster one's finer qualities, and now she must be going through a particular kind of hell that I don't like to imagine.'

Kate shuddered. 'Do you think,' she asked in a voice she managed to keep firm, 'do you think they may be holding her somewhere near?'

'Who can tell?' Professor Hatfield said. 'The bluffs and the woods continue through two whole counties on either side of the river. There are hundreds of square miles of wilderness at our doorstep. She may be out in some hut, or some lonely farmhouse or perhaps some cave; or she may

be far away by this time in a closed room in a big city.
But if we can once discover our man —'

His voice stopped as if it had been switched off. He
stood quite still, and his pressure on her arm tightened.
She glanced at him in surprise, and saw that he had turned
his head, that he was listening intently. Then she, too,
heard somewhere back in the woods a slight sound – was
it a footfall, the brushing of a twig?

Almost at once the professor resumed his walk along
the path, but he did not speak and she herself could not
bear to say anything just then. In a few minutes they had
reached the arch that led into the garden. There he paused
and peered out blinking into the brightness. Beyond the
flowers and the lawn, she could see June and Felix on
their horses, trotting up the drive, with little Bobbie loping
behind them. In the gay sunlight, with the sweeps of sky
overhead, the hills in the background, they were like the
figures in some old English print.

'I don't want to alarm you any further,' Professor Hatfield said with soft preciseness, speaking close to her ear,
'but I'm afraid now there's a new reason for you to be on
your guard. I have a strong suspicion, my dear, that someone was listening to our talk.'

Chapter Eight

KATE looked up with a start from the bench by the tennis court where she had just begun a letter to her, mother, and watched Jo as he came towards her out of the shrubbery that divided the court from the herb garden. There was no reason to be alarmed; here it was broad daylight; if she called, her voice would be heard on the terrace, or for that matter in the living-room; but since her talk with the professor this morning, she had tried to avoid being alone with anyone – with anyone but Ralph, that is; and Ralph, she felt, had for some reason been avoiding her. It was too horrible to think that among these people there might lurk the monster Professor Hatfield had described; and yet it was not so much fear that she felt as a kind of nervous incredulity. Just as a powerful electric charge may not injure when a weaker one would kill, so the very horror of the picture in her mind made it impossible for her to relate it, with real conviction, to any of these people, strange as they were, who made up the Valley Farms household.

· She had lived through the day like someone walking in his sleep; she would catch herself thinking trivial thoughts, making casual remarks, smiling or even laughing, as if this were a day like any other; then half waking, as it were, she would be swept along by such a sense of pity and horror that she wondered how she could think, or speak of anything except Clotilde – Clotilde and the all-enveloping nightmare of which her mutilation seemed only one part, one definite and ominous symptom. A few minutes ago she had finished two sets of tennis with June, whose strenuous game had badly beaten her and exhausted her wind. June was now in the house reading *Little Women*. After their tennis Kate had mentioned as tactfully as she could the reform of dress and make-up that Mr. Gladstone had suggested. June, who she was afraid might resent it, had jumped at the idea; she had insisted on fetching Kate her writing things so she would not have to move from her bench, and they had arranged a 'date' for a little beauty treatment before dinner. It was incongruous, perhaps, to consider such a thing to-day; and yet if you did not keep your mind well filled with trivia, if you let yourself wake up, you might plunge into a gulf, like the sleepwalker whom somebody disturbs as he picks his way serenely along eaves and over roof tops.

The shadow of the bluff, which had advanced across the whole width of the court, suggested already, so long before sunset, the furtive approach of evening. Kate could not bear to think that darkness once again would be crowding in from these hills, but as she watched Jo coming nearer she forced herself to smile. Her policy of avoiding people to-day had not been much help towards gathering clues for Professor Hatfield. She should really seek people out of her own accord. As she thought of the awfulness of Clotilde's position, she felt fiercely ashamed of her timidity.

'So here's where you are!' Jo exclaimed. 'Hidden away behind the trees, and I must say they make a lovely setting. I wish you could have seen yourself just now, as you looked up when you heard my step. It's too bad people have written so much about startled nymphs, so that the phrase stinks with banality; because really, you know, as you raised your head and tilted it to the side, with the breeze blowing back your hair so that I could see your ear, with your lips just parted, and the green leaves all around you — But of course you think this is only my line – rather quaint, rather foreign, just a shade middle-aged, eh?'

He stood in front of her bench and stared down at her

with a tight-lipped smile, his thick lashes so narrowed that she could hardly see the whites of his eyes.

She returned his smile. 'Not middle-aged', she said. 'Just quaint and foreign.'

As he laughed, she noticed the smallness, the evenness of his teeth; his blue-black hair, his intensely swarthy skin, gave his smile the brilliance of an Hawaiian's.

'May I sit down?' he asked. 'You wouldn't mind too much?'

'What makes you think I'd mind?'

'My dear Kate,' he said, 'you are innocent, yes, but you are no fool. You must have seen something of our situation here. You must have thought my own part was perhaps a shade equivocal; and it really was more than anything to explain my position that I was eager to talk to you to-day – as soon as I could.'

'You mustn't feel you have to explain anything', Kate said coldly. 'I don't think it's any of my business.'

He sat down beside her and hitched up his white trousers so that she could see his finely knitted cream-coloured socks.

'My little Kate,' he exclaimed, 'when you know me better, you'll realize that I never feel "I have to" do any-thing. The phrase is abhorrent to me. I am a musician, an artist; I need congenial surroundings to do my best work. If I could improve my playing, I would pimp without shame for a house of prostitution. My art comes first.'

'I've always heard,' Kate said, 'that too much comfort was apt to be a bad influence on an artist. It might make him lazy. It seems to me most of the great ones had quite a struggle.'

'Ah, but I am also a sensualist', he said. 'I love good food, good drinks, beautiful scenes and exquisite women. I love to receive pleasure; I love even more to give it, which is the refined essence of sensuality. If I can procure

7

some passing joy for Mavis, in return for what she, and her most understanding husband, my good friend Norman, can offer me, who am I to hold back? But, as I told you last night, I make distinctions. Mavis, Clotilde are bad women, and it is not merely a question of physical chastity. You, my dear Kate, are a good woman; no matter what you do, even should you be dragged through the gutter, you will always remain one. Last night, you may remember, I virtually pushed you from my room. I would not even go with you out into the darkness. It was no lack of admiration – quite the reverse. It was my homage to the immaculate.'

During his last words a chilling and incredible doubt had made it hard for Kate to maintain her smile; had Jo pushed her from his room yesterday evening so that he might be free to follow Clotilde into the shadows from which she had vanished? Had it occurred to him that his behaviour, if Kate thought of it afterward, might arouse her suspicions? Had all this talk of his just now, this unfolding of his character, been merely leading up to an excuse for his impatience to get rid of her? She felt that she must say something quickly or he would wonder at her silence. Then, with intense relief, she noticed that Mavis, in peacock-blue silk, with a rose stuck in the brassy halo of her hair, had appeared from the herb garden, and was watching them from under her raised eyebrows.

'So *there* you are!' she exclaimed. 'My dear Jo, I feel responsible for Kate while she is in my house, and I refuse to have her seduced before my eyes. Kate darling, don't listen to anything he says. The only time you can trust him is when he has his violin in his hands, and sometimes even then I think I should feel safer if he played the 'cello. But speaking of violins, Jo, my dove, I thought we were going to run through some sonatas before dinner. You've been playing so much lately with poor Clotilde that I'm afraid you are shamefully out of practice.'

Jo rose briskly from the bench. 'My precious Mavis,' he said, 'I was just coming to get you, but you can hardly blame me for lingering. A cup of pure spring water is delightful sometimes after even the choicest and oldest wine.'

He glanced down at Kate and laughed, and his face for a moment looked startlingly young and unguarded. 'Whatever else you may have learned,' he said, 'at least you will have gathered that I love to talk about myself.'

Kate watched them as they disappeared into the shrubbery, and noticed with a faint feeling of repulsion how Mavis managed to give this breezy tennis court, the wall of shadowed foliage, the air of a stage from which she was making her exit. Kate glanced up at the sky to catch once more the sense that she was out of doors. White brilliant towers of cloud were floating upward in the blue; it was the kind of afternoon that makes you think of kites flying, of flags waving. There were still some hours before darkness.

Then as she turned to pick up her writing pad, she saw from the tail of her eye a man's figure gliding from one of the poplars directly behind her to another one a few yards away.

Before she had time to be scared she recognized it as Ralph's. For a moment she felt slightly sick; Ralph was the last person she could have imagined eavesdropping and then sneaking off into the shadows.

'Ralph,' she called, 'I see you. Won't you come here?'

He came slowly towards her through the trees. His lips were set, but not in a smile; his dark heavy eyebrows were drawn together, as if to divert attention, by their fierceness, from the rest of his stricken face.

'I've come', he said. 'What did you want, Kate?'

'The first thing I want,' she said with a kind of desperation, 'is to know whether you are mad, Ralph, or whether it's I. I'm beginning to feel that perhaps we both are. But certainly you were listening just now to Jo and me.'

'Yes, I was,' he said gruffly, 'though I didn't hear much, if that's any consolation.'

Kate was far too bewildered to be angry. 'But why were you doing it, Ralph? I feel that everything and everyone around here is part of some plot, something confused and awful, the kind of thing you dream about, and now it turns out that you're in it too.'

'It's just because I feel the same way,' he said, 'I mean that there *is* a plot, that I was keeping my eye on you, Kate. It is confused and awful around here. I trust no one, unless perhaps Professor Hatfield, and really I don't much care what happens to anyone, anyone but you, that is. Certainly not to myself. They can go as far as they like, but damn them, they're not going to touch *you*!'

'They', she repeated. 'Who do you mean by "they", Ralph?'

'I don't know', he growled. 'I don't know a damn thing. That's part of the confusion.'

He turned, sat down on the bench beside her, and buried his face in his hands. 'Perhaps I am going mad', he said. 'It might be a welcome change. What's that kind of madness people get as an escape from an impossible situation?'

All at once Kate remembered the tone of Ralph's voice, the look on his face, when he had recognized that awful sticky hair as Clotilde's; and it struck her that her own feelings were unimportant.

'Ralph,' she said gently, 'it's very kind of you to look out for me – especially now.'

He raised his head from his hands and stared at her. ' "Especially now" !' he exclaimed. 'What do you mean, Kate?'

'I mean when you must be thinking so much of Clotilde. She seemed such a different kind of person from you, Ralph – you won't mind my saying this? – that I just couldn't realize you loved her so much.'

His stare fixed her more intensely; then to her amazement he laughed – but his voice was so hard, so dry, that it did not sound like his. 'You think I still love Clotilde!' he said. 'After you've seen her in her native haunts, after you've heard her talk? Where did you get that quaint idea?'

Kate felt that she might have replied: At any rate, you *are* engaged to her, but she knew it would seem unsympathetic. If she was more bewildered than ever, there was now, she realized, a sense of relief and thankfulness beneath her wonder: it was as if poor Ralph, no matter how desperate he might feel, had been suddenly set free from some airless underground prison. 'It's the way you looked when you recognized her hair', she said. 'I'll never forget your face.'

'I can well imagine that,' he said quickly, 'but do you know why, Kate? Of course the mere fact of its happening to anyone was hellish enough, but do you know why I felt a special kind of very personal hell? It was because during my walk yesterday night I was thinking how easy it would be for me to kill her. *There* would be action, I was thinking, and action of a most satisfying sort. In typical romantic fashion, I was mulling over ways and means when I heard that scream. Then when I heard it was Clotilde who had been attacked, it almost seemed to me as if I had willed it, as if my mind had cast a spell over her and now I was confronted with what I myself had done. It was a queer feeling, hard to explain, but I can't get over it, Kate. I wish to God I could!'

'I think I can understand how you felt,' Kate said, 'but Ralph dear, the reason you felt that way was just because it was something you couldn't possibly do. You'd never be able to commit a murder in this world: you're much too kind. You couldn't deliberately hurt anyone if your life depended on it.'

He gave her a long grave look. 'You think I couldn't commit murder?' he asked. 'You know me as little as that?'

She met his eyes, and as she stared searchingly into them, she saw that in their very gentleness there was something inflexible that might be more deadly than any mere excitement or fury, just because it would be always there. With a pang of terror, terror that was all for him, she realized that Ralph could kill, not for the sake of gain, not from fear or for revenge, but to exterminate something he knew was evil. Her conviction was such a shock that she felt actually faint; then, like fresh air pouring into a gas-filled room, came the certainty that if Ralph might be driven to murder, he could not be driven to cold-blooded cruelty; he couldn't have arranged a kidnapping and written that terrible letter; he could not have hacked off Clotilde's scalp.

Evidently he guessed something of her passing dread, for he gave her a sad smile touched with irony. 'You see?' he said quietly. 'You might as well know the worst.'

Kate still felt slightly dizzy. She glanced around her at the limpid green shadows over the grass, at the walls of rippled foliage, and then up at the dazzling spires of cloud pointing one above the other towards the deep free blue of the zenith. If only Ralph and she could escape into that upper freedom and break through the surface of the poisonous invisible water that filled this valley, then perhaps once more she could draw a normal breath.

'But if you feel that way about Clotilde,' she said after a pause, 'then why did you ask her to marry you?'

'Why indeed!' he exclaimed with his bitter laugh. 'You may well ask. Because I'm a romantic fool. Because I can't see the truth until my nose is rubbed in it. But to do Clotilde justice, she's very lovely to look at – that is, until you discover what's underneath that surface. She can be extremely charming and amusing when she wants to be.

She can even be pathetic. When I met her in New York, some awful men were after her. She told me, with the most discreet wistfulness, about her family. She asked my advice. She could be touchingly gay and give me the feeling that really she was desperate, but oh, so plucky! She made me think of her almost as a poor little princess surrounded by ogres, which was very flattering to me, because then I became the brave and noble young prince who might rescue her. It makes me want to vomit to think of it!'

He paused, and for that instant he looked as if there were actually something nauseating in his mouth. 'When I arrived at the farm,' he went on, 'it was barely a month ago, but it seems like years – I saw soon enough that if there were evil here, it was Clotilde's native element. By that time there were plans for the wedding and everything, but worse than that – and this is what I'm most ashamed of – she could still cast her spell over me at times. Oh, I wouldn't have gone through with it; I wasn't quite such a fool as that. I don't think she would have wanted to, herself. But she loved to torment me. The trouble was I let her know *I* wanted to back out. If she had thought I was still crazy about her, she most likely would have sent me packing.'

He wiped his face with his hand. Again Kate glanced up at the clouds and noticed with a faint shiver that a hint of the palest gold-colour had begun to stain their glittering whiteness. The sun, still high in the west, was slowly nearing the rim of these tufted hills.

'And then to see you!' he groaned. 'To have you appear like someone from a past life, the dear little Kate I remembered, only now grown up to be so beautiful – to have you find me here in this – this sty, among the rest of the pigs! That was the last twist of the knife!'

Kate reached forward and put her hand lightly on his knee. She could not bear to see him so wretched.

'Don't, Ralph', she exclaimed. 'You mustn't! Whatever Clotilde is has nothing to do with you. And whatever she has been, she's certainly paying for it now.'

'That's just it', he said in a sombre voice. 'What am I going to do when she comes back?'

'What are you going to do!' she exclaimed. 'You can go away from here and never see her again.'

'If she's returned sound and well,' he said, 'of course that's what I'll do. But suppose she's crippled, permanently injured in some way. Suppose her nerves are all shot to pieces.'

'I don't think that makes any difference', she said earnestly. 'I don't think it could ever be right to marry someone you hate – no matter what. I can't imagine anything worse, or more unfair, for both the husband and the wife.'

As he glanced at her with a slow smile, he seemed more like his natural self than he had been since yesterday evening at dinner.

'That's all very well for you,' he said, 'and I know you really think it, because you're fond of me. But unfortunately – or fortunately – I'm not very fond of myself, and so perhaps I can see the situation with more detachment.'

'Detachment!' she exclaimed. 'Is that what you call it? You *are* romantic, Ralph; that's the trouble with you. And if I can help it, you're not going to throw yourself away through some absurd notion of self-sacrifice. As far as I can see, it was just because Clotilde was clever enough to see how romantic you were, how you loved to rescue people, that she managed to get you in the first place.'

'At any rate,' he said, 'I don't have to meet the situation until it arises.'

Kate felt suddenly that she was blushing. Was it wrong of her, was it deceitful and underhand, for her to advise him in this way, when Clotilde was not here to defend herself? There was one thing at any rate that she could do:

from now on she must devote herself to Clotilde; she must shrink from nothing that might help Professor Hatfield rescue her a moment sooner. Because only by acting thus, could she prove to her own conscience that, much as she disliked Clotilde, much as she liked Ralph, she was not in her advice being treacherous and selfish.

Then as she thought of Professor Hatfield, she recalled the unseen prowler who had been listening to their morning's talk.

'Ralph,' she said, 'a little while ago you said that you were keeping watch over me to-day. Was it you in the woods this morning, by the summerhouse, when I was talking with Professor Hatfield?'

'No, it wasn't', he said. 'I only wish it had been. If anyone was spying on you, Kate – and I can well believe that somebody was – that only shows how careful you must be. You see that, don't you?'

She raised her eyes and again looked into his face, bent seriously towards hers. Then she saw his glance swerve, to pass over her shoulder, and realized that someone else had come from the house.

'There's June', he said. 'I'm glad at least I've got something off my chest. You've done me no end of good, much more than you can know. I'll be leaving you now, Kate, but I won't be far.'

He seized her hand and pressed it so firmly that it hurt. Then he strode off between the poplars, while Bobbie, who had been following June, tore after him, her stomach close to the ground, her head straining forward, like a tiny race-horse. Kate couldn't help smiling as she watched her; and then with a new surge of dizziness, as if she had stepped too near the edge of a cliff, she found herself wondering what Bobbie might bring back from her romp in those dark woods.

Chapter Nine

As she stood behind June an hour later and experimented with her thick black hair, Kate felt that she was learning, with surprising success, to cheat her sense of reality. When you could observe yourself doing something so frivolous, working at it as intensely as if it were of major importance, you could push really important things – your bewilderment, your pity, your terror – into the dim outer regions of your mind where you could only hope they would not gain new strength from their banishment, to spring on you, at some unguarded moment, with even greater fierceness.

She had decided she would bring June's hair softly back from her brow and temples, since it was just long enough to knot behind her head. Then, just for fun, she shadowed June's lashes, but so slightly that no one would suspect. She wiped off every trace of her lipstick, and although none of her own was an ideal shade for June's dark skin, she did have a scarlet one which looked at any rate better than the rose pink that June had chosen. June's dresses were discouraging; but Kate found a black one, ripped off some frilly white bows, and thus reduced it to something simple and inconspicuous. Then she stood off, by the door of June's room, and had June turn slowly around like a model, so that she could see the general effect.

What she saw was a young girl rather heavy and with plain features, but neither awkward-looking nor insignificant. You could see now the nice shape of her head; and her eyes with the help of Kate's handiwork were really striking and sombre. Kate smiled, and could feel at least that under ordinary circumstances she would have been delighted with both June and herself.

'You look wonderful!' she exclaimed. 'I just can't wait till they see you.'

June smiled back at her, and the scarlet lipstick, the simplicity of her smooth black hair, gave her smile a brilliance it had never had.

'Oh, Kate!' she exclaimed. 'Why didn't you come sooner? How happy we could be if everything wasn't so awful!'

'In a few days,' Kate said, 'perhaps tomorrow, everything will be over. And now, shall we go down?'

'Yes, let's. But there's something I think I ought to tell you first, Kate. You won't be angry with me?'

'How do I know,' Kate said, 'until you do? But I think you can take the chance.'

'It's just that Mavis has been talking', June said slowly. 'It made me angry, because it was about you and Ralph. When I came in from the tennis court she was talking to Father and Jo.'

Kate turned her head so that June would not notice how she had flushed. 'What on earth was she saying about Ralph and me?' she asked, and she had never tried harder to make her voice sound casual.

'She was saying – oh, horrid things. They were talking in the living-room and I heard them from the terrace. I almost rushed straight into the room and told her to shut up, but I was afraid you mightn't want me to. Should I have, Katey?'

'I'm glad you didn't', Kate said. 'But it makes me furious to think of it. What right has she to talk about us, I'd like to know, just because we're old friends?'

'I'm sure nobody believed her', June said. 'It's just that she's jealous of anyone young and pretty. She'd be jealous of me if I wasn't so ugly.'

'You're not ugly!' Kate exclaimed. 'You look stunning tonight. Wait till they see you downstairs.'

She went to June and put her arm around her waist; June had seemed so pathetic that it half diverted Kate from her anger with Mavis. After all, why should she be disturbed by the talk of an alcoholic and broken-down actress? She should have too much pride to let it bother her.

As the two girls walked downstairs, Kate thought of her afternoon's talk with Ralph; and the implications of something he had said struck her for the first time. If *he* had not been eavesdropping on Professor Hatfield and her, the list of possibilities had narrowed. She knew the professor did not believe the spy was a stranger. Who was he, then? It was not Ralph; it could not be Felix, because she had seen him the next moment a quarter of a mile away, riding up the drive with June. That left only Jo, Mavis, and Ruby, because she ruled out the Larsons entirely; and then, as June and she stepped from the living-room on to the terrace, she noticed Mr. Gladstone. Physically, it would have been possible, no doubt, for him to be there; but such an idea was fantastic. She dismissed it at once.

'Well!' Mr. Gladstone exclaimed. 'My dear June, you look amazingly smart. Is this Kate's doing?'

Kate could not help admiring the way his tone established at once the sense that this was a normal evening.

'It's a work of collaboration', she said.

'I don't see why you need sound so surprised', Mavis said. 'Naturally one would expect a daughter of mine to have distinction. June is just beginning to grow up, that is all. You're emerging at last from the awkward age, aren't you, darling?'

But what pleased Kate most was the look Ralph gave her; and with Mavis in mind she deliberately sent him her most affectionate and brightest smile.

As soon as the flurry of their entrance had passed, however, Kate could not help comparing this scene with the similar one of yesterday evening, when Clotilde had appeared, so lovely-looking and smooth, in her grey dress. There was the same shadow across the garden, the same dusky glow of cloth and petal, the same fragrance in the air; only tonight there still towered above the woods the peaks of this afternoon's clouds, no longer white but stained with the palest rose. Bobbie lay sprawled on her back at the edge of the terrace; her front feet were drawn up to her chest; her hind legs spread limply. At most times, Kate could not have resisted stooping and stroking the silky stomach, delicately pink and marked with a few spots like the drops shaken at random from a pen; but tonight, here on the terrace, she could not bear to: even poor little Bobbie had become part of the enchantment.

She turned her head as she realized that Felix stood beside her with the cocktails.

'Congratulations, Miss Kate,' he murmured, 'you've done a fine job. It's lucky, by the way, that you can keep your head, because it seems that both our young men have lost their hearts.'

She took a long sip of her cocktail. Her glance wandered over the garden. Then, as she saw Professor Hatfield walking towards them down one of the paths, she had the ghastly illusion that time had been turned back twenty-four hours, that presently Clotilde would appear, that the two of them, each with her best smile, would shake hands. She remembered how exquisitely silky and smooth Clotilde's hair had looked in the early evening light, and quickly drank the rest of her cocktail. Tonight she would take two – or three.

Dinner was confused and seemed to pass quickly. She was placed, this evening, between Jo and Mr. Gladstone and only half listened to what they said. She decided that nothing would induce her to go out on the terrace for coffee; and as they all were strolling through the living-room, she said good night, and explained that she was going upstairs to write letters.

In the hall she was stopped by Professor Hatfield, who had lingered behind the rest.

'Good night', he said. 'I hope you'll manage to sleep', and then he added, softly and clearly, though his lips hardly moved: 'Since our talk this morning was not private, I think it may be safer for Clotilde, and for you, if we are not seen together. But keep your eyes open.'

It was a relief to get to her room and close the door behind her. She turned on a lamp beside the chaise-longue and sat down wearily, with her writing pad in her lap. She could hear again the frogs from the river; and a whippoor-will was calling somewhere far away in the woods. She had never before taken so many cocktails and she still felt dizzy and somehow distinct from her surroundings, as if she were enclosed in a wavy film which made breathing a trifle difficult.

She opened her pad on her knees and wrote: 'Friday evening, 16 June. Dear Mother.'

But how should she continue? What should she say? If she told Mother now what had happened she would scare her to death, and yet it was almost impossible to describe this place and these people as if everything were safe and normal.

After a long pause she made her pen write: 'I came out here, as I'd planned, on Thursday, yesterday afternoon. I've been here now for hardly more than twenty-four hours, and yet it seems as if it had been days.' That was true enough, but then what?

There was a knock at the door. She was sure it must be June, and was glad that she would not have to finish her letter, although she did not feel like talking.

'Come in!' she said, and the next instant dropped her

pen in surprise, for it was not June who entered but Ruby.

'Why Ruby!' she exclaimed. 'What is it? Can I do anything for you?'

For a moment Ruby simply stared at her, and Kate noticed what handsome eyes she had; they were a bright blue, very clear and piercing, and seemed to be coldly sizing her up.

'Yes, I think you can', Ruby then said stiffly. 'That's why I'm here. It's for my own sake that I've come but if you'll listen to me, it may be for your sake as well. And don't think I'm meaning to be impertinent, because I'm not. I have nothing against you so far. But here's what I've got to say. Felix likes you. I know the signs. He used to be gadding about all the time, but lately he's settled down. I want him to stay settled. If he gets fresh with you, you put him in his place. Oh I know you think you will. I know you think I'm insulting you by the very idea! He's a servant. He wears a livery. He's forty years old. Lots of girls have thought things like that about lots of men, and then it was all different. I know my place. I wouldn't come to you like this if I didn't think you were reasonable. I wouldn't come either, if Felix was just an ordinary fellow. But Felix is quite a man!'

Her voice had kept on at a steady level but with an effect of growing intensity, until at her last words it seemed charged with a strange passion and pride. Kate had been so amazed and then so impressed by her manner that there was hardly room in her mind for anger. While she was still wondering what she should feel, what she should say, Ruby turned abruptly and left the room.

Chapter Ten

THE terrace extended in every direction as far as her
eye could see, but it was not out of doors; it was an
enormous hall or theatre, with clouds painted on the
ceiling. From far away on the rose-coloured horizon a
small black and white object was scurrying towards her;
its chill green shadow reached out indefinitely before it
and was already touching her feet. But this was no ordinary shadow; it was viscous, slimy, like the track of a slug;
it glued her feet to the ground so that she could not move.
She closed her eyes in agony; and as the softly scurrying
feet drew nearer, the shadow, instead of passing her, rose
within her body like the mercury in a thermometer, the
green cold slime in a pond, that presently would reach her
heart.

'Kate dear, you must play with Clotilde.'

It was Mother's voice so she knew that everything was
safe. Clotilde stood before her, a little girl of twelve, in a
white lace dress; she was the prettiest girl at the party,
prettier even than Kate. She shook her curls so disdain-
fully that Kate reached out her hand, although she knew
it was very wrong, and gave them a sharp pull. The bunch
of hair came right out of Clotilde's head; Kate was holding
it, all bloody and sticky, between her fingers. She stared
about her in horror. The only thing she could do was to
fling it into the cage, and both hyenas started toward it.
The tough pinkish skin on their long tight bodies twitched
greedily as if to shoo off flies. It wasn't a lock of hair, it
was a small bloody animal that she had thrown to the
hyenas. It was still half alive, it was trying to escape. She
must rescue it, she must get it before they reached it. But

how could she, for one of them, on its hind legs, was walking towards her, its head thrust forward, its dark mouth dripping and smiling. It was whispering slyly into her ear in its awful gobbling voice. She must scream as loud as she could so that she would not understand what it said; but the voice, gobbling and chuckling, grew louder and louder. She could not scream. She could not breathe.

Kate heard herself groaning and managed to fling back the sheets from about her face. Her nightgown stuck to her skin; she was still trembling. For a minute she lay quite still, her mind confused, trying to forget her dream. Then a sudden conviction startled her into wakefulness.

It had not been merely herself that she had heard; there had been some other sound.

She had no idea what it was or from what direction it had come – whether it was from near or far away, from inside the house or from out of the window; but she was sure that during her struggles to break out of her dream she had heard something.

She sat up in bed. A breeze stirred the curtains and lapped against her damp skin. The square of the window stood out vaguely in the light of the waning moon. She could hear a swish and ripple of leaves that reminded her of the sea, but that was all; even the frogs were silent; or perhaps it was the breeze that blew their voices away, across the river, into that wilderness of woods and swamps that Professor Hatfield had mentioned.

And then she thought of June. Could anything have happened to June?

She got out of bed, put on her slippers and dressing-gown, unlocked her door and peered into the hall. The house was completely silent.

She walked through the thick darkness to the door of June's room, guided by the dim oblong of the transom. She could imagine that the straw matting crinkled ever so

8

faintly beneath her feet. For a minute she listened intently, her ear close to the door, and then she could hear June's peaceful breathing. She tried the knob very gently, though she knew the door would be locked.

She had taken a few steps back towards her room when she stopped suddenly. There was that sound again, remote, indeterminate. It came now from below, from the ground floor – or perhaps it was a step on the stairs.

Kate felt a desperate urge to run into her room, to lock the door, to spring into bed and burrow beneath the sheets; but she hesitated. This might of course be something quite normal; Mr. Gladstone might be coming up from his study, or moving around in the lower hall, although she knew by the moon that it must be very late – around two or three o'clock. But again, this might have something to do with the kidnapping, something to do with Clotilde.

Professor Hatfield had urged her to keep her eyes open for anything in the least unusual; and certainly it was unusual for someone to be prowling about the house at this time of night. Might this person, whoever it was, be choosing this hour to meet his accomplice – might he even be going out, with food perhaps, to the cave or hut in which Clotilde lay bound? She recalled Professor Hatfield's words: 'If anything we unearth results in rescuing Clotilde a day, or even an hour sooner, it may mean the saving of her life, or perhaps her reason.' She remembered her vow this afternoon when she had told Ralph that he should not marry Clotilde. Now was her chance perhaps to discover something: if she could only find out who this man was, it might be the key to the plot. It would do no good to tell herself that she would follow him outside the house: she knew that no matter how firmly she decided, her feet, her legs, at the last moment would simply refuse to carry her; but at least she could walk to the top of the stairs; she could investigate that far. Here in the house she would be safe, and to run back to her room now would be an act of pure cowardice that she could never forgive herself.

She turned, walked to the end of this little passage, and looked out into the main hall. There was no light, and no one was coming upstairs; so she moved as quietly as she could past the closed white doors to the head of the stairway. She stood there for a moment, with one hand clutching the banister, her throat and tongue so parched that she felt she could not make a sound no matter what happened. Someone, she was sure, was moving about in the dark near the front door.

He was fumbling with the lock, that was what he was doing. She caught her breath as a small flashlight went on; but it was not turned in her direction: it remained focused upon the lock. She saw a man's fingers turning the key, which apparently tended to stick; then the light was shut off, the door opened, and a dim figure slipped out and closed it behind him.

If only she had asked Ralph where his room was! But now if she were going to be of any use, she could not wait even a moment. The man had not looked up; he had not seen her; there was no possible danger. There was just a chance that she could make out who he was in the moonlight. She ran softly down the stairs, crossed the hall, and forced herself to open the door, which was now unlocked.

Slowly she peered out into the night. The air was so damp and chilly that it reminded her of shipboard. In front of her the lawn was blanketed by a white mist perhaps a yard deep, from which the scattered trees rose like huge feathery haystacks. Low above the hills a dingy crescent was dissolving in a streak of rust-coloured sky. She looked in both directions along the façade of the house – and yes, there to the left, a man was skirting the wall, moving past the windows that opened from the living-room.

She stepped outside the door but kept her hand carefully on the knob. In the moonlight and the fog she could not tell whether he was short or tall, dark or light. 'Perhaps I should follow him,' she thought, 'I should track him down; that would be the brave thing to do; but I'm afraid I'm not cut out to be a heroine.'

At the corner of the house the man paused, and she saw that he was looking back; he had noticed her. He ducked into the mist. Under that thick white cover he might be groping his way back; he might even, bent double, be running towards her over the silent grass!

In wild panic she clutched at the doorknob; and then occurred perhaps the worst thing that had ever happened to her; the barely opened door swung to, shutting her out. She heard the latch click.

For a moment her fingers were too weak even to try the knob. Suppose it were an automatic lock. It was all she could do to resist an impulse to plunge madly into the fog, to crouch hidden somewhere, like a small night animal, in the depths of some thick tree. But the knob was turning as she pressed it; she heard again that faint click, the white panel gave suddenly and she almost fell in upon the carpet. Then breathlessly she slammed the door.

Her heart was pounding so hard that she felt she might be ill; so she walked across through the darkness to the stairway and sat down on the bottom step, until she could breathe naturally. For the first time it struck her that if she should arouse everyone, she might discover who the mysterious man was. But suppose it were Mr. Gladstone, who could not sleep and who had gone for a walk in the moonlight. Perhaps when he had seemed to stoop he had merely walked around the corner. Or perhaps, and this was more likely, the night prowler was Jo who had been with Mavis and had now returned to his cottage.

These thoughts reassured her. She rose from the step and walked upstairs, thankful that apparently no one had heard the door.

Then, just as she reached the top of the stairs, someone looming suddenly from the darkness, grasped her arm, and she gave a little choking scream.

'For God's sake, Kate, is that you?'

The voice was Ralph's, and she felt so relieved that for an instant she could not speak.

'What's happened?' he asked in a tone whose anxious sharpness made it sound almost fierce. 'How did you get here? Did anyone come into your room? Are you all right?'

'Yes', she said with a half-sob. 'I'm all right. I'll be all right in a minute. It's just that you scared me so.'

'Have you been outside?' he went on. 'Kate, you shouldn't have gone, not for any reason. I was sleeping very lightly; in fact I wasn't really asleep. I heard a door slam. I thought it was the front door, so I hurried out here. Then I saw your figure coming up the stairs. I didn't know who it might be.'

'I heard something too', she said. 'That's why I got up.' And she told him of the noise that had wakened her and the man she had seen. 'Do you think he could have been going to Clotilde?' she asked. 'Do you think he was part of the plot?'

'I don't know', he said grimly. 'It might be. If it was Jo or Felix, either one of them could be back in bed and apparently asleep by now. But I do know this, Kate. You ran a terrible risk going out as you did. You must give me your word that if you ever hear any other noises in the night, you'll stay in your room. Of course you'll keep your door locked. And if you notice anything, when you're up and about, that seems suspicious or strange, you must tell me at once. Why didn't you wake me just now?'

'It seems to me that's what I did,' she said, 'even if I

didn't mean to. I would have earlier, but I didn't know which was your room.'

'It's the room corresponding to yours, at the end of the opposite wing. I wish it wasn't so far away. Now Kate, do you promise to do as I've told you, no matter what you hear? If not, I warn you, I'll spend the rest of the night pacing the hall outside your door.'

'I promise that nothing will drag me out of my room again tonight', she said. 'You needn't worry.'

Her voice broke during her last words, and it was all she could do to keep from crying.

Without warning, he pulled her against him, and held her for a moment so close that she could hardly breathe. Then he let her go just as suddenly.

'This is a fine state of affairs', he said in a gruff voice. 'Out of the frying pan into the fire, I should say. I won't apologize. You're forgiving enough to laugh it off. But now I'm going to escort you to your door, Kate. No more of this lonely wandering for you.'

Kate hurried on ahead of him, shaken from so many emotions – fear, relief, and then surprise – that it never occurred to her to be angry or to pretend that she was. Presently they turned out of the main hall into the little side passage.

'Good night, Kate', he said, as they reached the end. 'I'll wait out here until you put on the light.'

But just then the light came on: they could see it through the transom. The door opened and June stood on the threshold, in pyjamas and a pink woolly wrapper.

'Oh Katey!' she exclaimed. 'I've been scared to death. I thought I heard you scream. I wasn't sure. You know how it is when you wake up suddenly. But I knew it was something, so I thought I'd go to your room, and then I found the door unlocked and went in, and you weren't there. I thought something awful might have happened to you.

And then I heard a man's voice. Of course I see now it was Ralph's. So I turned out the light again and locked the door. I was just trying to get up courage to go out to look for you.'

'I'm glad you didn't do that', Kate said. 'But I don't wonder you were scared. So would I have been.'

It occurred to her then that June would certainly think it odd to see Ralph and her roaming the house in their dressing-gowns at this time of night; she remembered what June had told her about Mavis' gossip and found that she was blushing.

'I thought I heard a noise', she explained. 'It was somewhere in the house. Ralph heard it too. We both started to explore to find out what it was and I ran into him in the dark. He scared me nearly to death. That's when you heard me scream.' For every reason it seemed better not to tell June about the man she had seen.

'Well, good night', Ralph said. 'Remember what I told you, Kate.'

Kate left the door open until he had rounded the corner; then as she closed it she turned to June. 'You poor thing!' she exclaimed. 'I should have left a note. It never occurred to me that you'd wake up and come to look for me. Of course that was all on account of my silly scream.'

'Oh, that's all right,' June said, 'now that you're back; but I wonder, Katey – would you mind if I slept in here, on the chaise-longue? Just for the rest of tonight? I think I'd feel easier somehow.'

'I *know* I'd feel easier', Kate said. 'I think it's a fine idea.'

But she lay awake for a long time after she heard June's slow breathing, because each time she approached the threshold of sleep she felt that dreams were ominously lying in wait for her, like ghosts within the rooms of an empty house; and she would have to struggle back, with what was left of her strength, before they caught her and dragged her inside.

Chapter Eleven

Kate did not wake up the next morning until after nine. June had left the room without disturbing her, and the blanket she had used as a covering was folded on the chaise-longue. The fact that she had not taken it with her suggested to Kate that June was perhaps planning to sleep here tonight as well; and Kate felt that for both their sakes this would be an excellent idea.

Before she got out of bed she realized that the air had changed during the early morning hours: it was quite still now, close and very humid; this would be a really hot day, the first of the summer.

When she stepped into the dining-room, twenty minutes later, she found everyone just finishing breakfast – even Mavis. Kate wondered what could have brought her down so early; and then with a catch of excitement she remembered that to-day was Saturday: it was this morning that the letter should arrive with instructions for the delivery of Clotilde's ransom. Yesterday the mail had not come until after eleven, but her own feeling of tension made her realize why Mavis should have found it impossible to lie in bed.

'I'm sorry to be late', Kate exclaimed. 'Of course nobody must wait for me.'

As they all looked up at her, she wondered whether Mavis and Mr. Gladstone had been told of her night's experience. There was an empty place between Mr. Gladstone and Ralph, which Kate suspected Ralph had managed to keep for her; she sat down quickly and hoped that she did not look too exhausted and drowsy.

'Will you have your eggs boiled or scrambled, miss?'

She glanced over her shoulder at Ruby's impassive face, and as she thought of their strange brief interview in her bedroom the night before, she had the feeling that this was not a real breakfast, that Ruby was not a real servant, that this all was taking place on the stage. It was not even a real stage, though; it was a stage in a dream, one of those unpleasant dreams in which you find yourself in the midst of a theatrical performance and haven't the least idea what your next lines are supposed to be.

In a minute Mavis rose from the table. 'If you'll excuse me,' she said, 'I think I'll step outside for a breath of air, if there's any to be had this morning. I rather doubt it. I've always found the sight of plates with egg drying on them peculiarly depressing. They give you such a very "morning after" feeling, without the consolation of there having been a "night before".'

She lingered a moment, with her hands resting on the back of her chair. She was wearing a pale-green housecoat of accordion-pleated chiffon, which gave the effect of at once clinging and bulging, and reminded Kate of the well-filled resilient skin of a tomato worm.

'Remember, Jo,' she said languidly, as if the heat were already overpowering her, 'we're going to do a little work on the César Franck presently. God knows, you need it!'

'In that case,' Jo said, 'I'll go and limber up my fingers. I didn't sleep very well' – he flashed a brilliant smile at Kate – 'and I feel I'm still moving in a dream, a most delightful dream.'

Mr. Gladstone also rose. 'If your dreams are delightful,' he grunted, 'I envy you. But perhaps you enjoy them more highly seasoned than the rest of us.'

June and Ralph both remained with her while Kate had her breakfast; then as they rose from the table, Ralph asked her to play tennis.

'Kate's going to play with *me*', June said. 'Aren't you, Kate?'

She spoke so possessively that Kate might have resented it if she had not remembered that probably no one else had ever paid her any attention.

'I'd love to,' Kate said, 'but I won't guarantee that I'll hold out for more than one set, if the morning gets much hotter.'

'I'll watch you', Ralph said, and the three of them went out together to the court.

Sunlight streamed down on the hard clay from a hazy whitish sky, and for the first time since her arrival at the farm Kate noticed a flat faint smell of mud from the river or the bottom lands. By the end of the first set, which June beat her 6–1, strands of hair were clinging to her cheeks and forehead. She looked at her watch; it was quarter past ten, the mail might arrive in less than an hour.

'Come along, Katey,' June called, 'you'll do better next time. You just haven't got warmed up yet.'

'Warmed up!' Kate exclaimed. 'If I got much warmer I'd melt away.'

She walked over to the bench where Ralph was sitting. '*You* ask June to play a set or two', she said in a low voice. 'I know she'd love to play with you. You'd give her a much better game.'

He made a slight face. 'All right,' he said, 'since you ask me to. But I never feel comfortable with June. She embarrasses me.'

'Don't be silly', she said sharply. 'Get up and play with her. Quickly! Or she'll know you don't want to.'

'Hey, June,' he called obediently, 'how about taking on someone your own size?'

With a slight scowl, June glanced at him and then at Kate; Kate guessed she suspected that his offer was not spontaneous; but after an instant her face cleared and she called back: 'Okay, if you want to. Two out of three.'

Kate watched them for a few minutes and wondered how they both could move with such energy under this intense white sun. The green circle of hills seemed to-day not so much to be holding in the damp as shutting out coolness and life. The shadow was retreating from the bench on which she sat; so she got up wearily and walked through the shrubbery into the herb garden.

Here the sharp smell of mint, tarragon and sage gave one the illusion that the air was less stagnant. A man in a tight blue jersey and black trousers was stooping over a border in the shadow of the further hedge. He stood up as she stepped out into the sun, and she saw that it was Felix, with a pair of scissors in one hand, a bunch of herbs in the other. He smiled and came forward jauntily to meet her. After Ruby's warning, she thought that perhaps she should not stay here, not so much because she was afraid of him as because she stood in awe of Ruby; but she felt more curious than ever to find out what he was really like.

She could see in this costume that he was certainly a fine figure of a man. She noticed for the first time how broad his neck was as it widened to join his shoulders, how slim and yet powerful were his waist and thighs. He suggested in the easy control of his movements a figure in a ballet, a sailor, or perhaps a Parisian Apache, sure of himself, disdainful, and yet somehow sympathetic. His face was the only thing that revealed his age.

'Good morning', he said. 'I guess you didn't know I was a chef as well as a chauffeur and a butler.'

'A chef!' she exclaimed. 'I thought Ruby was the cook.'

'Perhaps I should say an assistant chef', he went on. 'Ruby relies on me for some of the finishing touches. I make a speciality of herbs and spices. Just smell this bunch. Now I claim that this bouquet is better than any flowers you could mention.'

He handed her the bunch of herbs, and she put her nose into it. It was delicious, she had to admit, though rather too strong, and in this hot sunlight it almost made her head go round. She offered it to him again, but he shook his head and smiled.

'You keep it', he urged. 'I'd be honoured. Put it in water in your room and the whole place will smell good enough to eat.'

'Thank you', she said, and in spite of herself she felt flattered; then, almost furtively, she glanced at the windows of the house to see whether Ruby were watching.

But the next moment her attention was attracted by the first bars of the Franck sonata floating out, clear and soft, from the open windows of Jo's cottage, beyond the herb garden and across the green. It seemed to Kate that the musical phrase tinted this heavy white air with a shimmer of iridescence, and gave it, for the first time this morning, a suggestion of life. She realized that of course Mavis must be at the piano, and was surprised at how well she played, far better than Clotilde, with an almost professional power and finish.

It gave her a quite different picture of Mavis and of her relation with Jo. Obviously somewhere within her there still lurked real energy and talent. It made her at once much more of a person, more to be respected, more to be reckoned with in every way.

'What did Mrs. Gladstone do when she was on the stage?' she asked Felix. 'Do you know? Was she in musical comedy?'

'No', he said. 'She was in real plays – legitimate drama. Shakespeare and all that. I guess she was pretty good. When she first came out here, after her marriage, she used to recite sometimes for friends in the evenings, but that sort of petered out.'

'It must have been hard for her at first, to be so far away from everything', Kate said.

Felix looked thoughtful. 'Well,' he said after a minute, 'I guess it was and it wasn't. You see when she was still on the stage she began to have those dizzy spells of hers.' She glanced at him doubtfully, but his expression showed no trace of irony. 'I know several times she couldn't appear. I guess her career was about washed up when Mr. Gladstone came along. He was crazy about her for a year or so, and afterward – well, he was always very understanding about letting her have her friends around for company.'

'You mean friends like Jo?' Kate asked.

'Yes', he said. 'That's the idea.'

Now, for an instant, she did catch a suggestion of the invisible wink she had noticed the night before last as he handed her her cocktail; yet she couldn't be angry, because she was almost sure she must have imagined it.

'She used to have lots of friends when June was a little girl', he went on. 'Sometimes several at once. And Mr. Gladstone had *his* friends, too. Oh yes, we used to have pretty lively parties out here. It was all very free and easy.'

Poor Clotilde! Kate thought. No wonder Professor Hatfield said her bringing up left something to be desired. And poor little June!

She glanced again at her watch. It was now 10.32. She would finish the letter she had begun to Mother last night, and take it down to the mailbox by the front gate.

She said good-bye to Felix, went into the house and up to her room. The letter turned into the briefest note; but she promised she would write several pages the next time and would probably have some curious things to tell; that might suggest that startling events were occurring, and yet it should not alarm Mother. It was now quarter to eleven. Perhaps the mail had already arrived; someone might have brought it in from the box. Her heart began to beat faster, as it did sometimes when she entered a doctor's office. What would the new message from the kidnappers be?

With her letter in her hand, she went downstairs and out of the front door. Here Bobbie joined her, her muzzle covered with dirt, as if she had been digging, and together they started down the drive to the road. The sun by this time had burned through the morning haze, and the zenith was a pale opaque blue. The wooded hill in front of her was at once dull and shimmering; in this hot light it had lost all individuality, all interest. It was just a sample strip cut at random from the thousands of miles of forest left over from the primitive world, when man had not yet come down from the trees.

As she stepped through the white gateposts and went to put her letter in the box, beyond the swath of clipped grass, she noticed Bobbie flattening out her body and wriggling forward with little friendly whines towards the group of cedars to the left of the gate. The next moment a voice called her from the shadow and she saw Mr. Gladstone sitting on the bank.

'It's a little early for the mail,' he said, 'but I just thought I'd be on hand. Won't you join me? It's as cool here as it is anywhere.'

Kate went over and sat down on the grass beside him. She was glad of an excuse to linger. For the first time Mr. Gladstone, as he sat here waiting for the postman, with his heavy eyes turned to the stretch of road on which the car would appear, struck her as a pathetic figure.

'Sometimes he doesn't get here till noon,' he said, 'but God damn it, if he's late this morning —'

'I haven't had a chance to tell you,' Kate said after a minute, 'but I do realize how awful this suspense must be for you, Mr. Gladstone. When a thing like this happens, there's really nothing you can say.'

'My dear Kate,' he exclaimed, 'your coming is the one bright spot in this living hell. If only I didn't feel so god-damn guilty!'

'Guilty?' she asked, surprised and touched, 'why should you feel guilty?'

'I guess I didn't realize how much of the old-fashioned father there was in my bones', he said. 'I remember in Sunday School they used to tell us you'd get caught up with, if you let things slide too far – and now look at this! Out of the clear sky! I keep thinking and thinking ever since Clotilde went, what chance has the poor kid ever had? Why didn't you come out here ten years ago and take them both on, June and Clotilde? Then at least I could feel – O hell! Mavis used to think it was cute when Clotilde came downstairs in her nightgown and some of the prime bunch that used to hang around would give her the cherries from their cocktails. I wouldn't put it past Mavis if she saw all along what it would do to her, and I never troubled to put my foot down. Mavis hated her because she was so much prettier than June, her own child; and she always was ashamed of June because June was so much homelier than Clotilde.' He gave a bitter rumbling laugh. 'I'm afraid I can't get much credit for these moral qualms', he said. 'I'm afraid they are just a proof I'm growing senile, a reversion to childhood. You wouldn't suspect my father was a strait-laced Baptist, and I had all the advantages of a strict upbringing. In fact, I'm damn sure I'm growing senile. Here I am talking to the prettiest girl I've seen in a coon's age, and all I can think of is what a fine friend she'd be for my daughters. I apologize, my dear. You should have known me earlier.'

'I'm sure I like you better this way', Kate said.

He laughed again. 'Yes, I guess you would. You're soft-hearted, and there's always a kind of romantic interest about a piece of old debris – you know, the old men that

come to your door selling shoestrings; old broken-down
dogs, old horses. If I wasn't old day before yesterday, I am
now; and if you had met me at the height of my charm,
I'm afraid you'd have seen through me.'

Kate remembered her talk on the terrace, day before
yesterday, with Jo; and wondered if all men whose main
interest in life was women were obsessed by the idea of
growing old.

Before she could think of anything to say, Mr. Gladstone
was scrambling to his feet. 'I hear a car', he exclaimed.
'Don't you?'

Kate listened, and then realized that what had seemed
merely the shimmer of the noonday heat was actually the
sound of a faint throbbing; but it must have been at least
two minutes before a small car appeared from beyond the
curve in the road.

'That's he', Mr. Gladstone said, and his voice was now
matter-of-fact.

Kate watched him tensely as he took three or four letters
from the box and handed them to the postman. It seemed
to her that no postman had ever taken longer to sort out
the mail to be delivered; but at last he gave Mr. Gladstone a bundle of letters with a couple of magazines. Mr.
Gladstone thumbed through them.

'Sorry', he said to Kate. 'There's nothing for you.'

Kate was disappointed; she had hoped to hear from
Mother. Since tomorrow was Sunday, there would be no
delivery; and now she would have to wait until the day
after.

Mr. Gladstone picked out one letter from the pile and
stuck the rest into his pocket. 'I guess this is it, all right',
he said, and his tone was as calm as when he had announced the postman. 'If you'll excuse me for a minute —'

Kate watched him as he read it, his face impassive
except for the faintest scowl. She could see that it was

several pages long and printed in red on the same cheap paper as the others.

When he had finished, he folded it and stuck it in the pocket with the rest of the mail. He gave her a long thoughtful glance from under his dark lids but for the moment did not speak, and she hesitated to ask any questions.

'Kate,' he said at last, 'would you mind hunting up June, and then coming with her to my study? If you meet anyone else they'll be sure to ask you if the mail has come and if you know anything about the letter. You can just say that for the present I can tell no one what's in it.'

They walked up the driveway together without speaking. Mr. Gladstone went into the house, but Kate skirted off to the right with Bobbie, and cut through the garden to the tennis court. Ralph and June were still playing as vigorously as ever, though they both looked intensely hot.

As soon as they had finished a game, Kate called June, and June and Ralph both came quickly.

'The letter!' June exclaimed. 'It's come, hasn't it? Do you know what's in it?'

Kate shook her head. 'Your father wants to talk to you in the study', she said. 'I think we'd better go right off.'

'The letter *has* come?' Ralph asked.

'Yes, it's come', she admitted.

'Tell Mr. Gladstone,' he said, 'that if there's anything, of any sort, that I can do —'

'Yes, I will', she promised, and she was grateful to him for not asking any more questions or insisting on coming with them.

When they stepped into the study, a dark-panelled room with hunting prints on the walls and not too many books, Mr. Gladstone characteristically did not move except to raise his puffy bluish lids so that Kate and June could both catch the full force of his stare.

'I think you girls will be interested in this letter', he

9

remarked in a businesslike voice. 'When you've heard it, you will understand why I called you in. It's fairly long, so you'd better sit down, and make yourselves comfortable – if you can!'

Kate sat down in a huge leather easy chair and June perched on its arm, with her fingers touching Kate's shoulder.

Dear Mr. Gladstone,

Since you drove into Woodside this morning – that is, Friday, the 16th – I assume you were acting like the sensible business man I have taken you to be and were collecting the little matter of $50,000 which we had named as our fee. I know I can also assume that you are intelligent enough not to have marked the money in any way, or to have taken down the numbers. When I specified only small bills, I did this really for your sake, to save you from too severe a temptation, because I know how badly you would feel afterward, if any greedy desire to retrieve your cash or any unchristian yearning for personal vengeance, had led you to take a step which would result in most unpleasant things happening to one or both of your daughters. Needless to say, nonetheless, the bills will be very carefully examined, as a sound business precaution, before any steps are taken towards fulfilling our side of the contract, namely the handing over of your daughter Clotilde.

Now as to the way in which we demand the money shall be delivered. Wishing to spare your feelings as much as we can, I warn you that at first reading you may be slightly alarmed. You may even hesitate to carry out our directions. As to this latter point, we have merely to say that if you vary our specification in the faintest degree, the whole deal is off. As to the former, I think a little thought will convince you that the course we have marked out for you is not the result of idle whim, still less of any mean desire to torment you, but merely a sound and most understandable precaution.

To come to the point: we should like you to give the money, wrapped in an inconspicuous brown paper parcel, to your daughter June. She must start at two o'clock tomorrow afternoon, the afternoon of the day you will receive this, for the bluff about two miles below your farm, opposite the old ferry landing. Under the largest oak tree on that particular bluff – there is no mistaking the tree – there is a flat stone a trifle more than a foot across and roughly rectangular; under that stone she will find a note directing her to some other place. You see it will be a kind of a treasure hunt, and I hope she will be able to take it in the spirit of a game. In the second hiding-place she will find a second note, directing her still further. I will not say how many stations there may be, because in games of that sort part of the fun consists of the surprise, but in the final spot designated she will leave the package and will receive written directions as to when and where you are to call for Clotilde.

Since we realize that a jaunt of this sort may seem a trifle formidable for a young girl to take alone, she may, if she likes, take her young friend, Miss Katherine Archer, with her. You see, we are doing everything we can to make it easy for everyone. I assure you that June (and Miss Archer, if she cares to go) will be quite safe on their little hike so long as they obey the directions they will find, and so long as you yourself do nothing to endanger them. If we wished June any harm, at present, we certainly would not bother to lure her off into the wilds. You remember this was not necessary in Clotilde's case, nor would it be in hers. No, it simply occurred to us that this might be the simplest way of providing a hostage for your discretion until an hour or so after the money had been delivered.

N.B. On no account should the dog be allowed to follow.

One more word before closing. In our last letter, you may recall we criticized the methods of average kidnappers. It seems to us that in allowing only one chance to the bereaved family, as they so often do, they are unnecessarily brutal. Let me remind you, that if anything goes wrong, we promise you we will *not* kill Clotilde. Instead, before we touch June, you will receive next time perhaps Clotilde's hand. I say 'perhaps', because although we have talked over alternatives with Clotilde herself, we have not yet decided on the particular part that might prove most persuasive. We very much hope, however, in common humanity, that we have persuaded you sufficiently already, and that you will not require a second chance. In fact, we feel we can count on it.

As Mr. Gladstone's voice stopped, Kate felt that these dark walls were slowly revolving about her; it was as if the steady level of his reading were the only thing that had kept them still; she could feel June's fingers pressing into her shoulder, but she did not dare to look up at her, she did not dare even to move, for fear that she might burst out laughing or crying – or perhaps be sick. From another world she could hear faintly the violin and piano; the music no doubt had been going on all the time that Mr. Gladstone was reading but she noticed it only now. She noticed, too, that Mr. Gladstone was again looking at June and her with no change of feature.

'Well,' he said at length, 'I wanted you to hear it. I have no comments to make. The only fair thing is to leave it up to you.'

In the silence that followed, the room turned more and more slowly and finally stopped with a faint and nauseating lurch.

Then she heard June's voice: 'I'll go', she said. 'I'll have to go, but Kate mustn't. I won't drag her into it.'

'Of course I'll go. Don't be foolish!' Kate was relieved that her voice had spoken for her so promptly, because she could not have forced it just then.

'I think,' Mr. Gladstone said slowly, 'that there is no real risk. As the writer of the letter suggests, there would be no point in it. At least, I'm afraid the risk would be even greater if we didn't do what he asked. However, this doesn't apply to you, Kate. The letter doesn't require you to go, and you mustn't feel you have to keep June company on a mission of this sort. June has explored this region by herself since she learned to walk.'

'You can't imagine my not going, can you?' Kate asked, and now she felt that she had gained control of her voice.

'I'd have no right to think badly of you, if you didn't.'

'I feel it's more important what I'd think of myself', Kate said.

'Very well then', Mr. Gladstone exclaimed briskly. 'You're a damn good sport, and I'm not at all surprised. In the meanwhile don't mention this to anyone. Don't even let them know I've read you the letter. We want to guard against any well-meaning interference which actually, I think, just now, is the thing we have to dread most. If you will both come back to this room at about ten minutes to two, I'll give you the package.'

Chapter Twelve

IT was five minutes after two when Kate and June
stepped into the thicket of trees beyond the tennis court
on to a narrow steep path that Kate had not noticed before; and Kate felt almost at once that they had plunged
into the midst of the wilderness. It was hard to realize that
the farm, with its neat buildings, its lawns and its gardens,
could not be more than a few hundred yards away.

The woods were intensely silent; only in the distance she
could hear a drilling sound, which stopped, began again
and stopped, and which she knew must be a woodpecker
searching for grubs. The smell of leaf mould, of rotten
bark, of fungus, hung in the air as in a closed room. Each
leaf, each twig, was as motionless as if the whole forest
were a huge 'natural' background for a wild-life group
in a museum.

The trail grew steeper and steeper; and in a minute they
were scrambling upward, clinging to saplings and exposed roots, along the foot of a rocky ledge perhaps six
feet high, from the top of which a fringe of juniper branches
jutted out like a line of broad green-black eaves. Kate
found herself stooping instinctively, because this ledge reminded her of a picture in a fairy tale, a picture which
always had scared her as a child, in which a young man
climbed through a lonely forest, suspecting no danger,
while just above him, on an overhanging rock, an ogre
was crouching with a huge stone poised in his hands. She
was glad to step out a few minutes later into the glare on
the top of the bluff.

June, who had been a few yards ahead, now stood still
to wait for her. The package of money was in a knapsack

slung over her shoulder, along with two bottles of Coca-
Cola. When June, at the last moment, had gone back to
the icebox to get these, it had seemed to Kate that on this
particular excursion they would feel in no mood for drink-
ing cokes; but already she was thankful that they would
have something to drink before they reached home.

Kate climbed up through the sparse grass until she was
standing beside June. By now her eyes were used to the
brightness.

In front of her a series of terraces edged with yellow
rock descended for a hundred feet or more to a group of
gnarled junipers, which seemed from here to be hanging
over a void. Below, sparkled the broad whitish-blue river,
winding in either direction as far as the eye could see between bluffs whose bare tops protruded from a blanket of
forest. Wooded islands, close to either shore, were rimmed
with beaches of pink sand, along which at intervals there
gleamed with the paleness of bone the trunk of an up-
rooted tree, washed downstream by the floods of past
seasons. The whole landscape seemed to be trembling
under the heat and glare. At first glance she could not
discover a single house.

Then June pointed down to the left, where a small bluff,
not nearly so high as the one on which they stood, stuck
out into the river.

'There's where Professor Hatfield has his shack', she
said. 'Do you see it? About half-way up, just above those
white birches.'

'What a wonderful place to live!' she exclaimed. 'But
how does he ever get a bicycle up that hill?'

'He doesn't', June said. 'There's a lane that leads in to
the river from the main road. We'll be crossing it soon. He
leaves his bicycle at the edge of the lane in an old piano
box.'

They followed now, much more quickly, the top of the

bluff which kept on, rising and falling, for half a mile; then they climbed down into woods again, though the slope here was not so steep as it had been at first. In the hollow their path crossed at right angles a dirt wagon trail, raised above the marshy ground on either side. 'That's Professor Hatfield's lane', June said.

Here in the bottom lands the air was even heavier, and Kate had to keep brushing away swarms of small sticky gnats. She was glad when after ten minutes they began to climb once more, and presently came out on another bluff – a long dry ridge scattered with yellow verbena-like flowers that Kate did not recognize.

'There's the tree!' June said, pointing to a huge oak near the crest. 'That surely must be the one.'

Kate's heart beat faster as they walked up to the oak tree.

'Yes, there's the stone!' June exclaimed.

'It looks heavy', Kate said. 'Don't you want me to help you lift it?'

'Never mind', June said, and sliding her strong fingers under the edge she moved it to the side without effort.

There, pressed into the close-packed dirt, was a piece of folded paper. June picked it up, unfolded it, and held it out towards Kate, so that the two girls might read it together. It was printed in the same red crayon.

So far, so good [the note ran]. On the other side of this bluff you will meet a trail that leads towards the river. Watch carefully, because it's overgrown, and you might miss it. It would be unfortunate for Clotilde, and perhaps for you, if you didn't find it. When you reach the river bank, walk downstream for fifty yards. There you will come to the top of a narrow island about twenty feet from the bank. Wade out to the island. On the spit of sand at the lower tip there is a tree trunk, half

buried. Dig in the sand close to the exposed roots of the
tree and you will find a wooden box. In that you will
find your directions.

'I hope the water's not too deep', June said. 'I'm wet
enough already. At any rate it can't be awfully far.'

Once again they plunged down into the undergrowth.
The path here was really precipitous, and several times
Kate asked June for her hand. The trail at the bottom
oozed water as they followed it towards the river through
a tangle of elderberries and briars; small spotted frogs
jumped up from under their feet and plopped into the
pools that soaked the roots of the bushes. By the time they
reached the bank their feet were so wet that they decided
it was not worth while taking off their shoes and stockings
to cross to the island.

'The bottom looks as if it would be awfully slimy', June
said. 'You wait here. I'll go first and see how deep it is.'

She started wading at once, and Kate, who had pictured
their sinking into the water waist deep, was relieved to see
that it did not rise above June's knees. The water was
warm and muddy; the island was a thicket of small trees
bound together by wild-grape vines and brambles; they
kept to the beach, and after they had gone thirty yards
they found themselves on the spit which the letter had
described. There, sure enough, was the dead tree, silvery
white, with a network of twisted roots like a knot of snakes
in some East Indian carving.

Both girls got down on their knees in the coarse sand and
started scooping it up with their fingers. Kate was beginning to grow a little worried when her nails scraped something hard, and the next moment she uncovered a cigar
box. She opened it hurriedly, spread out the paper enclosed, and again June and she read the message together:

Go back to the main trail that leads from the river to the highway. Follow it in the direction away from the river for about half a mile. Then, to the right, before you reach the main road, you will see an abandoned house in an orchard. Enter the house, go upstairs, turn to the left and go into the front room. In a corner of the room there is a closet. Across the back of the closet is a deep shelf. On that shelf, in the extreme right-hand back corner you will find directions under a pile of loose plaster.

'That means we have to go back over that last bluff', June said. 'Are you as hot as I am? What do you say we drink our cokes now? Then I won't have to lug the bottles any further.'

They drank them sitting on the beach, with their backs resting against the dead tree. The bottles were lukewarm, and the brackish smell of the river seemed to flavour the drink, but even so Kate swallowed it greedily. The river slipped by on either side of them, washing bubbles on to the wet sand; two large herons pulled themselves up from another island, a hundred yards downstream, and flew with dangling legs across to the further bank to vanish among the trees. Where am I? Kate suddenly asked herself. What am I doing here? This strange errand has nothing to do with my life. And then, with a cold feeling about her heart, she had the conviction that she could never escape from this region in which she had been living (asleep or awake?) during the last few days, that she could never find her way back to the normal comfortable world she had always known.

'Gosh, I'm hot!' June exclaimed, as she put down her empty bottle. 'What do you say we take a dip, Kate? The water would be cleaner on the offshore side of the island.'

'Do you think we better?' Kate asked doubtfully.

'Oh, I only mean for a few minutes', June said. 'We've sure made good time so far.'

Kate stared at the sinuous current. Perhaps if she dived down through that shining water it would be like stepping back through the looking glass and she would find herself once more in the real world.

But it was just then that she heard a noise. It was so short that she did not know what it was – the crack of a twig, the swish of a branch, a footstep, from the thicket behind them in the centre of the island.

'Listen!' she exclaimed under her breath. 'Did you hear that?'

'What?' June asked.

'I don't know. But I think – It seems to me, June, that someone is on this island. Someone beside ourselves.'

'It might be some animal', June said, but Kate could see her dark skin turn a shade less swarthy.

'Yes, it might', Kate said. 'There! You must have heard it that time. It sounded nearer, I thought.'

'Yes, I heard it then', June said. 'Perhaps we better get going, after all.'

Without speaking, they waded back to the shore, and as they hurried along the swampy path there was complete silence all around them. But after they had reached the top of the bluff, they heard the sound again, this time down to the right among the trees, as if someone – or something, a wild beast, perhaps – were furtively trailing them.

'I don't like it!' Kate exclaimed, and she realized that if she were not careful there might be tears in her voice. 'I hate these faint sounds.'

'So do I', June said in a half-whisper. 'But I guess the only thing to do is to keep right on.'

'Of course', Kate admitted. 'There's nothing else to do.'

When they came to the trail at the foot of the bluff they

could go more quickly, for although it rose, the slope was comparatively gentle and the ground was smooth underfoot. As they pushed on through the woods, Kate tried to pretend that she no longer heard the noises, just as you may almost convince yourself that you no longer hear some ominous sound in the motor when you are driving a car; but she knew that whatever it was, it still prowled beside them. The air was so breathless that even the faintest rustle called attention to itself, like a stone flung into a pool.

'There's the house', June said at last. 'I remember I once explored it when I was little.'

Kate felt that she could not have kept on much longer.

They climbed over the wooden gate, which was chained and padlocked, and waded through the long grass of the yard. It was a small house of yellow brick set among old apple trees; at one end a lilac thicket grew as high as the second story windows. There were zigzag cracks in the walls, and the roof of the porch had fallen in. They had to climb over a litter of boards to reach the door.

The house was filled with hot green twilight like a sticky jelly. They could see no scrap of furniture. The floors looked rotten, and jagged bits of plaster lay everywhere.

'We must look out for the stairs', June said. 'I'll go first. If they'll bear my weight, they'll certainly bear yours.'

As she followed June cautiously up the steps, Kate thought what a perfect trap this would be.

In the upper hall they turned to the left, as directed, and entered what must have been the best bedroom. The door of the closet stood ajar. June went in, and Kate could hear the loose plaster falling as she brushed it aside; but all the time she was listening for some noise – the slightest creak of a board – downstairs. If she heard it she did not know what she would do: she must prepare herself not to scream. Or perhaps there would be no need for effort: her heart might simply stop beating.

'Here it is!' June said. 'Gosh, I hope they don't send us much further.'

When she came out of the closet there were pieces of plaster caught in her dark hair. This time the paper was not folded but crumpled into a tight ball, so that anyone discovering it would not suspect it contained a message. June spread it out carefully – there were three sheets covered with printing – and offered it to Kate.

'You read it to me', Kate said. If she were listening to June's voice, she couldn't keep straining her ears for noises downstairs.

> You have reached the end of your journey [June read]. Leave the parcel on the shelf where you found this. Be sure and cover it carefully with loose plaster. You are responsible for it until it is called for, so it would be most unfortunate if it was discovered by some tramp. As you know, you are now very near the main road, and you will be tempted to return home that way. Do not yield to that temptation. Go home by the trail through the woods and the river bluffs. There is no hurry. You can rest whenever you want to. We advise you to tell nobody where you left the money until Clotilde is returned. Of course you can use your own judgment, but if anyone, for any reason whatever, comes near this house while Clotilde is still in our custody, the deal is off, and your ramble will have been useless – not to speak of the money thrown away.
>
> *What follows is important:* tomorrow (Sunday) afternoon Mr. Gladstone and Mr. Green must drive into Woodside. At the square they are to turn left on State Highway 17. Keep on through Brookfield, Red Earth and Tuscoda. When they have driven twenty-one miles on 17 from the square in Woodside, they must keep their eyes open for a small road going down a hill into woods.

It is about two hundred yards beyond a barn that has recently burned down. At the bottom of the hill, at the edge of the woods is a stream. Follow the current, on foot, for three hundred yards. At that point there is an abandoned cabin. In the cabin they will find Clotilde, resting, comfortably we hope, on some straw. Don't be alarmed if she seems slightly drowsy. It has seemed more humane recently to keep her under the influence of a mild sedative.

Be sure and obey the directions to the letter. It will take two men to carry Clotilde back to the road, and who are more fitting for this purpose than her father and her fiancé?

We hope there will be no need for further correspondence.

June looked up at Kate, as she finished, and suddenly, before she could help it, Kate burst into tears.

'I don't think I can go back through those woods', she sobbed. 'I don't think I can!'

June flung her arms about her. 'We won't', she said. 'We'll go back by the road. We've left the money. Why shouldn't we? Damn them anyway, the damn fools!'

'No, no', Kate said, as soon as she could control her voice. 'This is crazy of me, June. It's just that I'm so tired. We must do exactly what it tells us to. And if that – that person hasn't hurt us so far, he probably won't. Perhaps he's gone away. Or perhaps, if it's one of them, he'll wait around for the money.'

'I'm sure it would be all right to take the road', June said, but now Kate would not hear of it.

As they went downstairs, swished through the grass in the yard, and climbed the gate, there was no sound anywhere to disturb them. It was easier walking down the trail than up, and Kate was just beginning to be convinced that the prowler had gone, when suddenly, not thirty feet ahead of them, a man stepped out of the woods.

Kate drew in her breath hysterically and clutched June's hand, but then, with a sense of overpowering relief, she recognized Professor Hatfield.

'Hullo there!' he called pleasantly. 'Taking a little walk? It's a pretty hot day for one.'

'Yes', June said. 'Kate and I have been exploring.'

If Professor Hatfield suspected what they had actually been doing, he gave no sign of it.

'May I join you?' he asked. 'I'll be going in your direction.'

'Oh do come with us', Kate exclaimed. 'We'd love to have you.'

She had been afraid that when they turned off the trail leading to his shack, he would keep straight on; but he did not leave them until they reached the top of the bluff directly above the farm.

'Perhaps I won't go down here,' he said, 'because it would only mean scrambling up again, but I'll wait a few minutes to give you time to get home.'

'You weren't —' Kate asked hesitantly, 'you weren't by any chance out on a little island earlier this afternoon? You weren't tracking us through the woods, were you?'

He chuckled. His small eyes peered at them quizzically.

'Dear me!' he exclaimed. 'That sounds very sinister, doesn't it? Sort of like Red Riding Hood's wolf. No, as a matter of fact, I'd been tramping about across the main highway. It was a pleasure to run into you children. Remember, Kate, you promised to come and see me sometime, you and June. I realize that my house is rather remote, but I'd do my best to provide entertainment.'

Chapter Thirteen

As KATE stood at the door beside June and watched the green car, with Ralph driving Mr. Gladstone, move off between the trees to the gate, she could hardly realize that in a few hours the suspense might be over. Faintly, from somewhere beyond the valley, she could hear the sound of bells. Farmers were no doubt driving along the roads, on this quiet Sunday, to afternoon service in the little churches hidden among the woods. Clotilde was kidnapped on Thursday evening, she thought incredulously: 'If they bring her back now, the whole thing will have taken less than three days.'

June pulled out her handkerchief and wiped the sweat from her forehead. The afternoon was again hot. Masses of cloud lay along the rim of the hills, as if they lacked the energy to rise into the thick, pale sky.

June yawned. 'I think I'll go up to my room and see if I can take a nap', she said. 'I hate to lie around waiting for them to get back, and there's nothing I feel like doing. I kept waking up last night. I guess you did, too, didn't you? You certainly were thrashing about.'

'I *have* slept better', Kate admitted. 'I'm sorry I disturbed you.'

'It wasn't you that disturbed me', June said.

'You'd better go back to your own bed tonight', Kate suggested. 'I'm sure it's much more comfortable.'

'Yes, I guess I will', June said. 'Damn this hot weather! I guess we'll have showers by evening.'

June turned and went slowly into the house. Kate wished there were some chance of sleeping herself; but she knew that the most she could expect would be a

144

stupefying half-sleep that skirted the border of nightmare.

She strolled down towards the gate and wondered why she felt so lonely; but no – she did not actually wonder; she knew quite well. Now that Ralph had gone she felt that she had lost her one protector, her one link with the healthy world beyond this valley. Of course there was doubtless no longer any need for protection; the ransom had been paid, Clotilde would be returned, the whole cruel business would be finished; but Kate just now could draw little comfort from that reasoning. Nothing, she felt, could ever break the dark and poisonous spell that brooded over this valley.

She paused outside the gate, in the white road, and caught her glance straying to the junipers in whose shade Mr. Gladstone had sought refuge yesterday morning. It would have been some consolation to find *him*, if she couldn't have Ralph. She had felt, during their talk down here, that she was just beginning to know him; she was touched by his sense of failure. Poor Mr. Gladstone, he was certainly being punished.

As she started walking up the drive, she noticed a man and a woman coming towards her from the direction of the house, and in a minute recognized them as Mr. and Mrs. Larson, dressed obviously in their Sunday clothes. Sooner or later she must get to know them, because she was sure she would like them. June, who was such a friend of theirs, would help her in that.

'Hullo', she said now. 'You must have lots of energy starting off for a walk in this heat.'

'We're going to church', Mrs. Larson said with a suggestion of reproof.

Mr. Larson grinned. 'Trust her!' he exclaimed. 'If she lets me off in the morning, she gets me in the afternoon. She used to try to get me both times, but she's just about given that up.'

10

Mrs. Larson allowed herself the faintest smile. 'Now Olaf,' she said, 'don't you be fresh with the young lady. Don't you be acting like Felix.'

'I'm coming to see you sometime soon', Kate said. 'That is, if you will let me.'

'Just tell me in time,' Mrs. Larson said, 'and I'll make some nice Norwegian coffeecake.'

As she approached the house, Kate was half sorry she had met them; she had almost forgotten about them; she hadn't thought of their being around, but now she could not help thinking of their having gone away, like Mr. Gladstone and Ralph. Just now Kate would even have been glad to see Mavis; but Mavis had not appeared at lunch; she had kept to her room because, so Ruby announced, she had a 'sick headache'.

Kate skirted the front of the house, avoided the terrace, and walked into the garden. The sunlight was both harsh and veiled, and seemed to neutralize the tints of even the most brilliant flowers, so that the whole scene suggested a picture postcard. A small yellow wasp buzzed around her face, and she shook her head, not daring to brush it aside with her hand. From very far away, hardly louder than the buzz of the wasp, came the muffled growl of thunder. It might have been the caving in of huge vaults deep underground. Perhaps, she thought, when miners are trapped at the end of some close passage, the first crumbling of the shaft that blocks their escape to air and light sounds something like that.

She strolled back towards the terrace, then swerved and wandered through the shrubbery into the herb garden. She hardly knew whether she hoped or dreaded to meet Felix, as she had done yesterday morning; but Felix was not there.

It came as a relief when she heard a phrase on Jo's violin. It sounded like Mozart, but the sharp vaguely irritating smell of the herbs seemed to give it a hidden insistent meaning that had nothing to do with itself. It might have been an incantation.

She walked through the break in the hedge that led out on to the green in front of Jo's cottage. In a moment the violin stopped and Jo himself appeared in his front door.

'Wonderful!' he exclaimed. 'You come as an answer to prayer. I was going through some sonatas with Mavis this afternoon, and of course she is ill, bless her soul, though I suspect she will be herself again tomorrow. Come in, do! You say you have played all the Mozarts. We will not practise. It is far too hot. We will simply read.'

'I'd love to', Kate said. Nothing, it seemed, would make this dreadful period of waiting pass more quickly than playing Mozart sonatas.

They went through the long one in B flat, of which she was especially fond, and then tried the next one, in E flat. Kate did not feel so much at home in this one but on the whole it seemed to go well. When they had finished the last variation in the finale, Jo placed his violin on the piano, and wiped his face and neck with a huge handkerchief of orange silk.

'It is so hot!' he exclaimed. 'I'm afraid I can't keep my mind entirely on the music, even on Mozart. A day like to-day we should dress like *him*, eh?' And he glanced up at St. Sebastian above the fireplace, bound to his tree, with a cloth about his loins, his body bristling with arrows.

'He doesn't look very comfortable', Kate said.

'I imagine,' Jo said, 'that in his ecstasy he could feel no pain. I could understand that. "Love's arrows" is no mere pretty figure of speech. Like so many poetic figures that have come down through the ages, and so become meaningless to us, it is based on intimate personal experience.'

Kate felt slightly uncomfortable. Jo was standing close

behind her. There was a moment of silence, and again she heard, as far away as ever, the subterranean roll of thunder.

She got up from the piano bench and turned so that she could see him. He was staring at her with a fixed smile, his teeth tightly clenched.

'I have an idea', he said, as she walked away from him across the room. 'A wonderful idea! It is too hot to play any more – at least to make music. Why not go swimming, you and I?'

Kate smiled with relief at this very normal suggestion, though nothing would have induced her to go swimming now with Jo.

'I'm afraid we'd get so warm climbing back over the bluff that it wouldn't be worth while', she said.

'Ah, of course, but we don't have to go over the bluff. If one follows upstream through the woods for about a mile this bluff peters out into nothing. There is a lovely little beach, and at this season the river is still cool.'

'It sounds awfully nice,' she admitted, 'but I really haven't the energy this afternoon. And besides, I didn't bring my bathing suit out here. It never occurred to me.'

'But I have no bathing suit either!' he exclaimed. 'We would not need them. No one comes to that beach. This does not shock you, I hope, you who are an artist. It is a question of milieu. For grown men to go swimming in crowds in stuffy pools without even wearing trunks, the way your American men do, I find very distasteful. It always seems to me unpleasantly promiscuous and crude and at the same time slightly naïve. But for a young man in his prime, or hardly past it, and an exquisite young girl, to go swimming in a river, in the midst of the wilderness, to let themselves drift beneath overhanging boughs, to splash each other among the reeds – it would be very primitive and very beautiful and very innocent.'

Kate would have laughed if she had not felt so uneasy. This suggestion was one of the things you make a note of to be amused at later but which at the time are anything but amusing. The smell of the herbs seeped faintly into this hot room; and as she noticed it, the odour seemed to vibrate with an effect of iridescence, so that at one moment it was mint she smelled, then sage, then tarragon. Jo was walking restlessly about.

'Well', he asked. 'You'll come? Yes?' He stood and faced her, his head thrust slightly forward, the same tight smile on his lips.

'No', she said, and tried to smile naturally. 'I certainly will not. I never felt less like a nymph.'

'Ah,' he exclaimed, 'but I never felt more like Pan!'

He was standing between her and the door, and now he came slowly towards her, his arms outstretched, his black eyes fixed on hers, as if he would hypnotize her.

She looked desperately around, as if to decide which way to run, and then suddenly the complete assurance of his smile made her so angry that she did not even try to escape. Instead she waited for him to get within a yard of her, and then struck him sharply across his cheek.

'Ouch!' he exclaimed, and raised his hand to his face.

'Jo', she said fiercely. 'Stop acting like a fool!'

He stepped backward, still rubbing his cheek.

'I hope my jaw doesn't swell', he said with an anxious air which was such a contrast to his manner of a moment ago that she had to restrain an hysterical giggle. 'It would be very awkward holding the violin.'

'If it does, it's your own fault', she said.

He looked at her with a tentative smile, as if he were testing his facial muscles.

'Yes', he admitted. 'It was my fault. It was foolish. It was a lapse from grace, such as even the saints sometimes experienced. But this still close air, with thunder in the distance, I find it has a strangely aphrodisiac effect. It is some consolation to realize how quick my responses still are when subjected to adequate stimulus. Kate, my dear, you fierce tenderhearted virgin, if you will not come with me, then I must go by myself; and after I have soaked in that cold current for fifteen minutes you will find me once more as respectful as a worshipper before a Madonna. I hope this doesn't mean we can't have any more music together this month.'

'Why shouldn't we have music?' she asked; but as she stepped out on to the green, she decided that after this she would be careful of the time she chose for it.

Ahead of her, from the direction of the big house, she heard Bobbie whining; she peered into the dense immobile shadow and presently discovered her, tied by a leash to a cherry tree near the back door. She went over to her, stooped, took her head, gracious and sleek as a young fawn's, between her fingers, and kneaded the folds of her throat. Kate would have liked to let her loose, but did not quite dare.

'Good-bye, Kate', she heard Jo call, and looking over her shoulder, she saw him, with soap and towel in his hand, walking along the edge of the woods. 'If I am drowned,' he went on, 'say a prayer for a lost soul.'

He stepped into the fringe of trees and was gone.

Until the moment of his disappearance, Kate would not have believed that she could miss Jo; but now she would have been glad to see him return. It was as if everybody were creeping away, one by one, according to some devious and furtive plan, as people might steal from a city at the rumour of plague. The whole farm, with its gardens, its great lawns, was beginning to take on the air of emptiness, of stealthy waiting, that had chilled her the other evening after she had played with Jo, and Clotilde had vanished. The harsh afternoon light seemed almost more treacherous than the darkness, just because it speciously appeared to be so frank. Again she heard thunder beyond the hills, and now it suggested a long sleepy growl from the depths of the jungle.

She felt suddenly that she must see June. Perhaps the music had wakened her; but even if June were still asleep, Kate would sit in her room, so that she could feel that someone, someone she trusted, was near. She said good-bye to Bobbie, went in the back door, through the empty kitchen, and then hurried upstairs. Perhaps it would not be too selfish to wake June: she had been lying down for nearly an hour.

Kate hesitated by the closed door. Suppose it were locked, should she tap on the white panelling? But the door was not locked. She stepped into the room and looked at once towards the bed. The pillow showed a depression where June's head had lain, but June herself was not there.

Kate had to check a desire to burst into tears. Of course June might be in the bathroom across the hall. Kate went out quickly, tried the bathroom door; it opened to reveal another empty room.

But June might have gone downstairs to find *her*; June might have been walking through the living-room, or the garden, at the very moment when she herself was coming in the back way and climbing the stairs. Kate ran along the hallway and downstairs once more: there was no one in the living-room; there was no one on the terrace.

She stared out over the crude neutral brightness of the garden. 'June,' she called, 'June, where are you?' and she realized that her voice was hushed, as if something that lay in wait in the thick depths of this breathless afternoon must not be allowed to hear.

She ran down across the grass and through the poplars to the tennis court; then back through the herb garden to the green behind the house where she had started. Bobbie was still there, tied to the tree; but there was no one else.

Where was Felix? She must find him at once. Something awful, something that she could not bear to think of, might be happening to June. She went into the kitchen and looked around. It was somewhere back of the kitchen that Ruby and Felix had their rooms. Beside the refrigerator a door stood ajar. She peered into the room beyond: it was only a pantry, but beyond it there was another door, and this one was closed.

She knocked sharply and listened. After a minute, with a mixture of relief and dread, she heard someone moving about. The next instant the door opened, and she was standing face to face with Ruby, who was wearing an old kimono and who looked half asleep.

'Where's Felix?' Kate asked quickly. 'I've got to see him.'

Ruby blinked and stared at her suspiciously. 'And just why have you got to see my husband?' she demanded.

Kate was too frightened now to get angry. 'June has disappeared', she said. 'I can't find her anywhere.'

'What's the excitement?' Ruby asked. 'June took care of herself all right before you got here. There's lots of places she could be.'

'I know,' Kate said, trying now to keep back her tears, 'but don't you see, at this time, when this awful thing has happened to Clotilde, when June got that letter —?'

'If that's the way you feel,' Ruby said, 'why didn't you keep an eye on her yourself? I'm not paid to look after June. Neither is Felix.'

Kate met Ruby's stony glance with a feeling of hopelessness. Then a wave of anger swept over her, carrying away even the realization of her terror.

'I won't argue with you', she said fiercely. 'Tell me where Felix is, and don't waste any more time.'

Ruby's glance did not waver; her expression did not change.

'If you must know,' she said, 'though I don't see it's any of your business, Felix has gone fishing.'

'Whereabouts? Is he somewhere near?'

'He's somewhere along the river', Ruby said with a trace of an ironic smile. 'He may be upstream, he may be downstream. He may be near, he may be far. But let me give you one piece of advice. Not even Felix likes a woman along when he's fishing.'

Before Kate could say anything else, Ruby had closed the door in her face.

For a minute Kate could only stand there, while her anger, her sense of injustice, rose within her like a searing hot geyser, shaking her body, bringing tears to her eyes; then it left her empty, for her sense of panic to rush back, to take possession of her trembling and make it its own. And mingled with her fear now, her fear for June and for herself which was one inseparable feeling, was a new sense of guilt. It was quite true; Ruby and Felix had not been paid to keep their eye on June; neither had she, of course; but in accepting Mr. Gladstone's invitation she had in a measure assumed that responsibility, and to-day of all days she had left her. Could Jo's asking her to make music with him be part of a cold-blooded scheme? Was it meant to keep her busy while June was spirited away?

She ran through the pantry and the kitchen into the dining-room. She called once more, desperately: 'June! –June!' She could not bear to call again, because the house seemed so deathly still after her voice had stopped. Besides, what was the use? She knew June was not in this house.

But Mavis was. Even though Mavis was the last person you could count on, she must be told at once; she was June's mother. Kate remembered how beautifully she had played the Cézar Franck; perhaps Mavis, after all, would surprise her.

Kate walked upstairs, tapping lightly on the banister with her fingers to break the silence, and knocked at the door of Mavis' room. No one answered. She turned the knob gently, the door opened, and Kate saw that the shades were drawn so that the room was filled with a sultry orange dusk. She could hear now an irregular stertorous breathing.

'Mrs. Gladstone', she called. 'Mavis! I'm sorry to disturb you, but I simply have to.'

The breathing paused for a second, and continued as before. Kate walked over to the bed.

Mavis was lying on her back, her head wrapped tightly in a towel. She had no make-up on, and her face was a uniform putty colour, except for the flanges of her nose which Kate could see, now that they were bare of powder, were congested by a network of small veins. Her mouth lolled open. Even without bending over her, Kate could smell the stale stench of gin which coiled around her like an invisible fog. Mavis, too, in her own fashion, had gone away, like the others.

Kate turned from the bed. She must get out of this house at once. But where could she go? What could she do?

Then she thought of Professor Hatfield. He would be the one of all others to consult. He would know what to do, if anybody did. Fortunately she had seen just where he lived, and the bluffs, the woods themselves were not so terrifying as this empty house, the dull glare of these lawns and gardens. But even if the woods lay under the blackest enchantment, she must brave them now, because it was June she must think of – only of June.

She hurried downstairs, and in the hall it occurred to her that she could take Bobbie with her; that would be some company at least. But rather than go through the kitchen and perhaps run into Ruby, she went out through the living-room, and around by the terrace and the herb garden. As she was untying Bobbie's leash, it struck her that perhaps Bobbie had been tied up so that she could not follow June.

With Bobbie straining at the leash, Kate hurried through the bushes to the tennis court and the wooded path that led to the crest of the bluff. If only Professor Hatfield were waiting at the top, as he had been yesterday when June and she had come down! Bobbie seemed to know the path well, for she went clambering ahead, stopping now and then to sniff the black leaf mould, to explore a juniper bush or a heap of pine needles. When Kate came to the overhanging ledge which she had noticed yesterday, she almost turned back; as she passed quickly under its fringe of junipers she began talking to Bobbie to keep herself from thinking of what might be lurking above. The thunder was now almost continuous but it sounded as far away as ever; she could imagine its curdling this soggy green air among the trees, as it was said to curdle milk.

When she reached the short grass at the top, Kate was out of breath, and stood still a minute to look around her. The light over the sprawling river, with its sand bars and islands, over the miles of forest and bluff, was paler than yesterday; but straight ahead of her the most distant hills, and the sky above them, were a dense livid blue. As she watched that dark horizon, a pink-white flame flared up for an instant and brought into relief the volutes of nearer clouds.

She felt some small thing hit her ankles, and looking down saw that Bobbie was digging in a patch of dirt and gravel about a yard from where she was standing.

'Come along, Bobbie,' she said, 'we must be getting on.'

She tightened the leash and gave it a little jerk, but

Bobbie paid no attention. She kept up her excited digging and scratching, her muzzle buried in the dirt, her paws sending up a steady spray behind her.

'There's nothing there, Bobbie', she said. 'That's not a rabbit hole.'

But the next moment she leaned forward with an awful feeling in her stomach and throat: there *was* something there – beneath the dry yellow surface there was something clotted and dark, a kind of red-brown paste that made an irregular stain more than a foot across. She gave such a sharp pull on the leash that Bobbie was lifted backward on to her hind legs, and almost fell over.

'Bobbie', she called. 'Don't! Come here, Bobbie!' And she dragged Bobbie along towards the rim of the first terrace from which the bluff began dropping towards the river.

Then all at once Bobbie ran swiftly ahead, with excited whines and barks. The leash did not quite reach to the little cliff, and she strained and jerked at the end more violently than before, her front feet pawing the air as if she were swimming against a strong current.

'What is it?' Kate asked. 'What are you after?' And as she stepped forward, Bobbie ran to the edge of the terrace and stretched her neck down as far as she could, with her same little whines.

Kate leaned over, herself. The crumbly yellow rock dropped almost sheer for about eight feet, and beneath was a grassy ledge a few yards wide, and then another miniature cliff.

'June!' Kate called breathlessly. 'June dear, are you there? Are you hurt? Is it June, Bobbie? Is that why you're so eager?'

She looked along the top of the ledge to see how she could get down, and a few yards to the left she saw a half-dead cedar growing on the ledge below and reaching a few feet above the top of the cliff. It would be possible to climb down with its help.

Bobbie followed her in tense excitement as she walked quickly to it. 'No, Bobbie', she said. 'I can't take you. It's hard enough for me alone. You'll have to wait up there.'

Then as carefully as she could she let herself down between the scratchy grey branches, and in a minute or so she was standing on the ledge below, and staring up at Bobbie's slim little head just out of reach.

Beyond the cedar tree the ledge narrowed swiftly and soon disappeared; but in the other direction it continued on a level around a curve in the main contour of the bluff. Kate walked in this direction, and when she reached the curve she saw that the cliff now overhung considerably, so that she would be invisible to anyone standing above.

Another cedar tree grew close to the rock, just beyond, and as she passed it she saw that she was standing at the entrance to a cave, one of the caves of which June and Professor Hatfield had spoken. But this was not a real cave: it was nothing but a stretch of grass, and then dirt, sloping steeply downward and backward for fifteen feet beneath the overhanging cliff; and even from where she stood, Kate could see something wrapped in a blanket lying on the ground at the bottom.

'June!' she called desperately. 'June!' But she knew that if this was June she could not answer her.

She scrambled down the slope, knelt by the bundle, and pulled back the top fold of the blanket. As she did so, she noticed a faint smell, at once sweetish and nauseating, as if from the slimes of some poisonous fungus.

The face she stared at was not June's; for the last instant she had known it could not be. If it were not for the clotted tangle of silvery-gold hair she would not have recognized those bruised and swollen features – that throat with the blackish grooves in the flesh, where strong fingers had pressed and dug into the larynx until death had come.

'Clotilde!' she gasped. 'Clotilde!'

She drew in her breath sharply. The faint smell seemed to line her mouth and throat, to penetrate to the centre of her brain. She must struggle or it would paralyse her thoughts.

Then she was aware that something had changed; a bar of shadow lay across the blanket where it wrapped Clotilde's legs. It did not move, and for an instant she tried to tell herself that it had been there from the first. But there had been nothing at the mouth of the cave to cast a shadow.

She forced herself, very slowly, to turn her head. A man's figure was outlined against the sky at the cave's entrance.

'No!' she called wildly, without thinking of what she said. 'No! No! You mustn't!'

The man did not advance from where he stood. Only his head jerked forward to peer down at her, with a swift hyena-like movement.

Chapter Fourteen

'You seem to have discovered something.'

Not until he spoke did Kate recognize the man as Felix. His voice did not sound quite natural; its smoothness seemed hardly to conceal a kind of chuckle and snarl. He was stripped to the waist, and his whole chest and torso bristled with patches of reddish hair so thick that it looked as if his body might once have been covered with fur, like a wild beast's, and that the blotches of pale tight skin showing through were merely where the fur had worn off, or been eaten away by the spread of some scurf or mange. Even when she looked at his face, smooth and gleaming with sweat as it peered down at her, it was hard to think of this man as the debonair Felix she remembered.

She tried to tell herself that she should feel relieved, that it was all right, that there was no need for panic, but even so she could hardly force herself to speak. She must swallow; she must do something to overcome this paralysis of her throat and chest.

'Yes', she said finally, in a queer flat voice. 'It's Clotilde. She's been murdered.'

'Murdered? How can that be? Mr. Gladstone and your friend Green have gone to rescue her.'

'But it *is* Clotilde!' she said. 'She's been strangled. It must have been right away.'

'Right away?'

'Right away after she was kidnapped.'

'What makes you think so?'

'Because – because she must have been dead for several days.'

Felix lifted his head and sniffed the air. She had grown

used to looking at him now, outlined against the light-
filled sky, and she could make out his features more
clearly; she could see that his eyes were half closed, that
his nostrils moved like an animal's. She remembered that
hyenas made their dens in cliffs and fed on carrion.

'Yes, perhaps', he said; and again his head jerked forward. As his eyes focused upon her once more, it seemed
to her that he was smiling. 'And so you think she's been
strangled?' he asked. 'That's a very brutal way to kill, but
I suppose it's practical. Once someone has his fingers
pressing against your windpipe, you can't make much
noise. In fact there's not much of anything you can do.'

'No', she said faintly. 'No, there's not.'

She drew in her breath once more and cowered backward as he took several steps down the slope into the cave;
but after he had come a couple of yards he stopped and
crouched on his heels on a ledge of stone that broke the
steep incline, like a landing. Now that the sky was no
longer behind him, she could see his red-brown eyes fixed
upon her with a gaze that was at once soft and sly; she
could see the faint rise and fall of his chest beneath its
thatch of sticky hair. He had not threatened her; he had
not suggested in any way that she could not leave the cave
whenever she wanted to; but from where he was crouching
he blocked the middle of the entrance, and she could not
bear to take a step towards him, to try to get out of this
place with its faint numbing stench of the grave, for fear
of the awful moment when he would stretch out his arm
to stop her. At least so far she could not be sure she was a
prisoner; she knew that she could not be sure, because if
she were, her heart would swell and swell until it filled her
whole breast, until she could not breathe and would die
of pure terror.

'Hasn't it struck you,' he asked after a minute, 'that it
was a pretty dangerous thing to go looking for Clotilde?

If the murderer left the body here, he must have hoped it wouldn't be found just yet. If he had caught you here, he might have felt he had to – well, shall we say, make some arrangements.'

'I wasn't looking for Clotilde', she said, and although he was not more than ten feet away, she wondered whether her voice would reach him. 'I was looking for June.'

'That would be just as risky,' he said, 'and just as useless. If June is gone, I'm afraid there is not much you could do for her either.'

'Where is June?' she asked. 'Do you know where she is? I must find her.'

This time she was sure he smiled. 'Who knows?' he said. 'She might be in another cave wrapped in a blanket. Let's hope that's not the case.'

'Will you come with me, to look for her?'

An agonizing gust of hope fluttered for an instant in her breast as she stared up at him.

'I must cool off a little,' he said, 'before I do anything else. As you can see, I'm very warm. I've been exercising. When the air is as heavy as it is this afternoon, and charged with electricity, it's apt to be oppressive, or don't you think so? Of course it's exciting too. You kind of feel that anything may happen.'

And now again Kate was aware of the soft persistent thunder, like some huge animal growling to itself as it thrust its muzzle deep into the warm entrails of its prey.

'It's too bad you didn't bring the herbs I gave you along', he went on. 'We could have used them in here, couldn't we? Did you put them in a vase in your bedroom? I kind of liked to think that you would be smelling them as you lay in bed. I even flattered myself they might remind you of me. If the murderer found you here, it would have been sort of hard on him, poor chap, to find such a beautiful girl – to have to make arrangements for her. It would seem such a waste, wouldn't it? I think he'd try to get all the fun he could first. And then perhaps, who knows, if he was a well-set-up fellow, if he knew his stuff, there might be no need for final arrangements. That seems hardly possible, but you can never tell with girls, and he must be the kind of fellow that takes a bit of a risk now and then. It might be worth it. Who can tell?'

As she crouched on the small ledge, he had been balancing himself by the tips of his fingers touching the stone on either side of him; and now she noticed that he was slowly pushing himself up. His head stretched forward, swaying slightly, and the muscles moved in his arms and shoulders.

Then he sprang to his feet and looked around as Bobbie scurried, tumbling over herself, down the slope to the bottom of the cave and thrust her paws into Kate's lap, her tail wagging frantically. The next moment another shadow pointed downward across the dirt to where Kate was kneeling, and Kate staring up at the sky recognized Professor Hatfield.

'Well, well', he exclaimed cheerfully. 'This is a surprise! I wondered why Bobbie seemed so excited.'

'I'm glad you turned up, Professor', Felix said. 'Miss Kate here has discovered that Clotilde has been strangled. She found the body. It's down there, she says, wrapped in that blanket. I was telling her it would have been a risky thing if the murderer had been hanging round the neighbourhood and had trapped her here in this cave.'

Felix had not moved from where he stood; the timbre of his voice had hardly changed; and yet he was once more the respectful though somewhat independent Felix she knew, the man who had driven her out to the farm, who had gallantly offered her the bunch of herbs. He was shaggier than she would have expected, but that was the only difference. For a moment it seemed to her that she had been imagining things or that the shock of finding Clotilde's body had unhinged her mind temporarily; but then as she recalled the soft insistent gloating of his eyes as his glance moved over her body not more than a minute ago, she knew only too well that she had been suffering from no delusion.

'So poor Clotilde was murdered!' Professor Hatfield exclaimed gently. 'I half suspected it.'

He walked down into the cave past Felix, knelt beside Kate, and stared for a long moment at Clotilde's face. Then he bent still nearer, and Kate turned away her head as she realized that he was examining the awful dark grooves in the throat.

'Hmmm!' he murmured. 'I can see a few shreds of black lint or something of the sort in the marks made by the murderer's fingers. It looks as if he had worn black gloves.'

'I suppose now,' Felix said, 'there's no longer any reason for not calling the police. I didn't like to leave Miss Kate here alone, and she seemed so upset by what she had found, and I don't wonder, that I thought she better have a chance to catch her breath for a few minutes before she tried the path.'

'That was very thoughtful of you', Professor Hatfield said. 'Yes, I agree with you, we should certainly now get in touch with the police as soon as possible.'

'Should we try to take the body down?' Felix asked. 'I guess you and I could make it all right.'

'I don't think it should be moved', Professor Hatfield said. 'They will want to find it just as it was left.'

'Well then,' Felix suggested, 'why don't I run right back to the farm and tell Mr. Gladstone, if he's got home, the poor man. If not, I'll call the police department in Woodside.'

'An excellent idea!' Professor Hatfield said. 'We'll be along shortly. I think Kate still feels a trifle uncertain, don't you, my dear? I'm sorry I haven't a good shot of brandy to give you.'

Kate did not answer. It was such a relief to see Felix walk out of the cave that she was afraid she might burst into tears. She saw that Professor Hatfield had taken a small penknife from his pocket and was carefully removing what looked like a shred of black worsted from a crease in the swollen throat. She turned her head away.

'There's plenty left for the police', Professor Hatfield said with an air of apology. 'But I thought I'd like to have a sample of this myself, just in case I should happen to come across a pair of black gloves. And now, my dear, if you feel strong enough, I think we might move at any rate out on to the ledge. This cave is not particularly inviting just now.'

He helped Kate to her feet, and reached down to take the end of Bobbie's lead. 'Don't be afraid to lean on me', he said. 'You still look rather pale, my dear.'

As Kate stepped out with him into the crude light on the ledge, she wondered if she would have a phobia about enclosed places for the rest of her life. She looked in either direction along the strip of sparse sunlit grass to make sure that Felix had gone.

'He's the man!' she then said tensely. 'He's one of the murderers.'

'You mean Felix?' Professor Hatfield asked.

'Yes. I'm sure of it.'

'I shouldn't be surprised', the professor said. 'But would you tell me why you think so, my dear?'

'The things he said. The way he looked. He all but admitted it. It was horrible.'

'Under the circumstances,' Professor Hatfield said, 'I think it's just as well that I arrived when I did. But my dear Kate, how did you ever find the cave?'

'It was Bobbie really', she explained. 'I came up on the

bluff because I was going to your house, on account of June.'

'June?' he asked. 'What's the matter with June?'

'She disappeared. I've been almost forgetting it because I've been so scared myself. But June has gone. She went up to take a nap and I foolishly played some sonatas with Jo. Then Jo left to go swimming and when I went up to find June she wasn't there. Do you suppose – do you suppose that Felix has murdered her too?'

'I'm sure he hasn't', Professor Hatfield said. 'I wouldn't worry too much about her now. I think you'll find she merely took a walk in the neighbourhood. As a matter of fact, before I turned up a minute ago, I had been watching Felix for some time. He was down near the river, in a little thicket from which I've often watched aquatic birds. He had no idea, I might say, that I was watching *him*. What interested me was what he was doing. He was digging an oblong hole in the ground, which is rather loose and sandy just there. It was perhaps five-feet six or so long, a couple of feet wide, and when he left, it was a good four feet deep. You may be sure he's been busy since lunch time. No wonder he looked hot just now.'

'Was it – was it a grave?' she asked.

'That's what I was following him up the bluff to discover', he said. 'But since I still didn't want him to see me, I let him have a good head start. Then when I saw Bobbie up on top, I kind of suspected you or June might be around, and I thought I'd better make haste.'

'But mightn't one of the others have gone off with June?' she asked, only half relieved. 'One of the accomplices from outside?'

'I'm quite sure now there were no accomplices from outside', he said. 'For the last day or so I've been coming more and more to that conclusion, and finding Clotilde's body here just about proves it.'

'But I don't understand', Kate said. 'I don't see that it proves anything.'

'Let's go up to the top of the bluff,' Professor Hatfield suggested, 'where the air is a little fresher. Then you can sit down and rest for a few minutes, and I'll tell you what I mean. Once we get back to the farm the police will be arriving and everything will be in confusion.'

'But what about Felix? Won't he be escaping?'

'You may be sure that Felix is not the kind of man to get in a panic and give himself away, just because he suspects *you* suspect he's the murderer. At the present moment he's probably telephoning the police. Or perhaps he's telling June, who no doubt was just as worried about you as you were about her, that you are in safe hands.'

They had been walking slowly along the ledge and now they reached the old cedar which Kate had climbed down. Mr. Hatfield helped her up through the twisted grey branches, handed Bobbie to her, and then climbed up briskly himself.

As he seated himself beside Bobbie and her in the grass, he drew a long breath. 'That's better!' he exclaimed. 'I shouldn't wonder if that storm reached us eventually, but perhaps not for an hour or so.'

Kate saw that the band of blue-black cloud had climbed up the sky; in contrast to its darkness, the nearer woods, just beyond the river, looked brighter than before, shining with a brassy glow; and she could see chains of lightning forking down into the hills like the tongues of snakes. There was a slight coolness in the air, and the thunder reminded her now of the boom of surf.

'I can tell you very quickly how things happened,' he went on, 'and then you won't have to worry any more, for either yourself or June; because you may be sure even if it's impossible to pin anything on Felix, and I think there's enough already to arrest him, that he won't try anything more just now. You see, my dear, he must have lain in wait for Clotilde somewhere near the house, very likely in the bushes between Jo's cottage and the terrace. He seized her throat from behind. The markings make that quite clear; you can see the pressure of the fingers from both hands on the windpipe. Felix is an exceptionally powerful man. He could have grasped her throat so suddenly and with such violence that she could make no sound. There were signs of hæmorrhage where his nails must have torn partly through the fingers of the gloves and broken the skin, and that shows how tightly they pressed into her throat. You and Jo were no doubt still playing at the time, and even if there had been a slight gasp, you would not have heard it.'

Kate tried to suppress the tremor that ran through her body as she thought that this had been happening to Clotilde at the very time when she herself had been so sure that Clotilde was standing close behind her, looking at the music. She still must have been hearing the sonata, floating softly through the night, when violence had sprung upon her out of the darkness and her mind had reeled in a spasm of agony and terror.

'Once he thought she was dead,' Mr. Hatfield continued serenely, 'he must have carried her up here. For a man of Felix's strength that would not have been difficult. The blood that Bobbie uncovered undoubtedly marks the place where he hacked off her scalp. I hope that bleeding does not mean that perhaps even then she was still alive. You remember I spoke the other day of the type of mind that would do such a thing without a qualm. No doubt he was rather proud of what fatuously must have seemed to him his original idea; but it was mainly for practical reasons: he wanted to scare Mr. Gladstone so much by this warning that he would not notify the police and would deliver the ransom in the manner specified. And you see, it worked. The hitch, of course, was that he hadn't realized that Bobbie had followed him. When she snatched the scalp, he must have been desperate. Probably what he had meant to do was to bury the body somewhere in the bottom lands. He might have flung it in the river, but I doubt it, because the current is apt to wash things ashore, and the water sinks so low in prolonged droughts that even a weighted corpse might come to light. No, I'm quite sure he was going to bury it, as he was starting to do this afternoon, and then the scalp lock would have been delivered at the same time with the note, perhaps flung into the window of Mr. Gladstone's study.

'But he realized then that Bobbie would probably run home with her treasure, that it might be discovered at once, and that he must not be suspiciously absent. So he dropped the body over this little cliff, still wrapped in the blanket that he must have had with him in his ambush, and shoved it down into the bottom of that cave until he could come back and put it permanently out of sight. And now you see why I'm sure there was no outside accomplice. If there had been, he never would have left the body here. When Felix went back to the farm, the other man would have disposed of it in some safe place. Perhaps Felix didn't think he could even wait to put it in the cave when he saw Bobbie running off. He may only have managed it afterward when he ran into the woods with Ralph and Jo, pretending to search for the mysterious man who threw the letter.'

'I was going to ask you about that', Kate said. 'You see there must have been another man. There must have been an outsider to throw that letter into the garden. You remember Mavis saw him.'

As she had been listening to Professor Hatfield's even voice, talking of this crime with the mild detachment with which he might have discussed a problem in mathematics,

Kate had felt herself growing more calm; she was even able now to look at that frightful waiting in the cave as a thing that had happened and now was finished, that could not happen again and so had lost something of its terror. Probably, she thought, this is the very best treatment anyone could give me to prevent that experience developing into some kind of complex, and she felt she would be grateful to Mr. Hatfield as long as she lived.

He smiled at her now, as if he were delighted at her objection. 'Ah,' he said, 'that was just the impression the episode was meant to convey. It's a fine example of impromptu tactics, of taking immediate advantage of an unforeseen situation.'

She could even return his smile, as she crumpled Bobbie's ears, and sniffed the coolness of the approaching storm.

'I must be very stupid,' she said, 'but I don't see what you mean.'

'You say the letter was flung in from outside, by someone lurking in the shadows, but the fact is that none of us saw any such thing. All we saw was the letter lying in the grass just beyond the edge of the garden, at the foot of the little slope that leads down to the garden from the terrace where we were all standing. It might have been flung from any point of the compass.'

'But if anyone had flung it from the terrace,' she said, 'somebody would surely have seen him do it.'

'Ah, there's where you're wrong', he exclaimed, and raised his finger as in the gentlest reproof at such inaccuracy. 'We were all so excited at that moment, and so confused, that he could doubtless have done it undetected at almost any time. He could have taken it carefully from his pocket, wrapped in a handkerchief to prevent fingerprints, and with a flick of his wrist, he could have shied it on to the lawn behind him. It was hardly twenty feet, you remember, from the edge of the terrace, and the envelope was weighted with a splinter of sandstone – no doubt to be flung, as I suggested a moment ago, through some window. But Felix was waiting for the perfect chance, waiting quite coldly, I imagine, but tensely so. And then when Mavis saw something in the shadows, something that attracted our attention, he seized the perfect opportunity.'

'But Mavis saw a man', Kate said. 'Do you think she was lying?'

'Mavis perhaps persuaded herself she saw a man', he admitted. 'A man just then would be the most dramatic thing to see, and Mavis is not averse to dramatics, especially if she can play a leading rôle. But Mavis did not say she saw a man. I remember her phrase because it struck me at the time. She said she saw something "dark and swooping", and for the moment I thought of course she had seen one of the beautiful owls that I'm so fond of. But I was probably the only person who thought that, and I only thought it for a moment. Mavis pointed off to the right of the sundial. We were all staring in that direction, trying to see if we also could make out something moving in that darkness, which was, moreover, the general direction from which you said Bobbie had come. Then, the next instant, we saw the letter lying on the grass to the left, near the poplars that hide the tennis court. We then naturally assumed that the moving thing Mavis had seen must have been a man, that he had flung the letter the moment before Mavis had noticed him. In fact I recall thinking that it was perhaps the swift movement of his arm that she had seen which would account for the strange adjective "swooping". But during the minute or so that our attention was attracted to the far corner of the garden, Felix could almost have walked out on to the grass and placed the letter there by hand without anyone's noticing. As for shying it from behind him, there was nothing to it. It

was child's play. Not that I have the least doubt,' he continued with his dry smile, 'that if the police question Mavis
on the subject, she will swear that she not only saw the
man, but saw him fling the letter, saw the curve it described in the air from the time it left his fingers to the
second later when it landed on the grass.'

Kate tried to recall the scene as accurately as she could
but everything that had happened so soon after the shock
of discovering the scalp remained a little confused, as if
she had been half asleep.

'Yes,' she said doubtfully, after a minute, 'yes, I can
see that it might have been that way. I'm sure it was, if
you think so, because you see things so clearly. But then,
what about the next night? If Felix was so nicely fixed —
But of course you don't know about my experience.'

'Yes I do', he said. 'Ralph told me. We've been sort of
working together these last two days. That only helps to
prove my point. Felix *was* nicely fixed for the moment, but
he still had the problem of disposing of Clotilde's body.
Even granting that it was improbable anyone would come
across it for a day or so – although I quite well might have
– it would be noticed before long by anyone who came to
the top of the bluff. And that hot humid weather yesterday
couldn't have made him feel any more comfortable. He
didn't quite dare go out again that same night. He knew
that people wouldn't be sleeping well. I doubt if Mr. Gladstone slept at all. And the next day was just as bad. If he
had been gone from his work for several hours, people
would have wondered. He chose the night, or rather the
small hours of the morning. Unluckily for him, you woke
up. You heard something and investigated and I compliment you on your nerve. You see, your trip downstairs
wasn't in vain, after all; if Felix had not been put off,
Clotilde's body might never have been discovered. When
he saw you watching him by the front door, Felix, you

may be sure, scuttled around the house and in the back
door to his room. For all he knew, you might waken everybody and the house might be searched. That was Friday
night. I doubt if he would have started up yesterday, because by then he may have realized that he was being
watched.'

'Were you watching him then?' she asked. 'Did you
suspect him already?'

'I've been watching everyone at some time or another',
he said, smiling. 'I was watching you and June, and I'm
afraid I gave you quite a scare, but after all it was for your
own good. And Ralph was helping me. I'd sort of deputed
him to keep an eye on Felix. I think Felix may have suspected what Ralph was up to, and that was why he specified that Ralph should go with Mr. Gladstone to call for
Clotilde. And Sunday was a good day, too. He could go off
fishing by the river without doing anything unusual. He
probably felt pretty sure of himself at last. It must have
been something of a shock when he found you in the
cave, and still more of one when I walked in. The only
thing he could do was to bluff, and I must say he did it
admirably.'

Professor Hatfield scrambled to his feet. 'I suppose we
had better go down now', he said. 'Mr. Gladstone may
have got back, and in a little while we'll be having to
answer questions from the police. I hope it won't be too
much of a strain, my dear. I hope you feel a little better.
Here, let me help you.'

He took her hands and pulled her lightly to her feet.

'I feel much better', she said. 'I don't think I'll mind
the police. It's Mr. Gladstone that I can't bear to see.'

They walked over the crest of the bluff, turned to take
a last look at the storm, and then started down through
the trees.

'The greatest relief,' she said presently, 'is to know who

it is, and to know they will surely get him. The kind of things I hate most are things that happen mysteriously.'

They had reached the little ledge of rock that skirted the path, and she felt that now for the first time she could walk under it without stooping or hurrying. But Bobbie, whom they had taken off her leash, had run ahead, and now was beginning to whimper.

Kate peered through the black-green shadow under the junipers to see what she was doing. The next moment, swaying, she reached backward and caught Professor Hatfield's hand.

Felix's body lay sprawled on its face, head downward, along the path, his skull split wide open so that through the mess of blood she could see the pale convolutions of his brain.

Chapter Fifteen

A GALE had swept down into the valley, the thunder was banging among the hills, and the first drops of rain were beginning to fall, when between crashes Kate heard a car stopping in front of the house. Professor Hatfield and she hurried to the door. It was not the police, whom the professor had notified half an hour ago, but Mr. Gladstone and Ralph; and Kate could hardly measure her relief when she saw that June was with them.

'Will you tell Mr. Gladstone about Clotilde?' she asked quickly. 'I don't think I could bear to.'

She had broken the news of Felix's death to Ruby, and she was still haunted by the sudden deadening of her face: it was as if her life's blood had frozen in that moment, to leave her a ghost, moving in a world of shadows.

'You say he's lying on the path to the bluff?' she had asked.

'Yes,' Kate said gently, 'but I don't think you better go there, Ruby.'

'He belonged to me,' Ruby said, 'in spite of all of them. I've stood a lot from him. I guess I can stand this.'

When Kate told Professor Hatfield where Ruby had gone, the professor had looked faintly disturbed. 'I hope she doesn't change anything,' he said, 'though I think I observed pretty carefully how things were. I'm afraid she may get rather wet if she stays out there too long.'

'I don't think she would mind that just now', Kate said. 'I don't think she'll mind much of anything ever again.'

And now as she watched Mr. Gladstone get out of the car, with the wind-lashed trees on the pale lawn behind him, with lightning shooting down into the hills and thunder rolling about the sky, it seemed to her that he too was a ghost.

'She wasn't there', he said, as he stepped into the hall. 'There was no burned-down barn within miles. There was no stream and no cabin. The whole thing was a god-damned hoax.' He swept his hand across his face, as if to wipe off the rain that had splashed it. 'It certainly looks,' he said, 'as if we'll never see her again.'

Professor Hatfield took his arm and led him into the living-room. Ralph, harassed and sombre, walked after them. Kate seized June's hand and pressed it impulsively.

'At least *you're* all right!' she exclaimed. 'Where were you, June? I was so afraid they'd got you too.'

'I found I couldn't sleep', June said. 'I might have known. So presently I came downstairs and looked for you. You were playing the piano with Jo. I didn't like to butt in, and I just couldn't sit still, so I thought I'd walk up the road towards town to meet Father and Clotilde. Father picked me up near the top of the hill. He's in quite a state. But I just can't believe that Clotilde is dead, Katey. Do you think they've taken her somewhere far away? Do you think they will send another note?'

'I don't think there will be any more notes', Kate said. She flung her arm across June's shoulder, and led her to the stairs. 'Let's go up to my room', she went on. 'Awful things have happened this afternoon, June dear, and I must tell you about them. Professor Hatfield is going to tell your father and Ralph.'

When they stepped into Kate's bedroom, the rain was falling in such dense sheets that it almost wiped out Jo's cottage and the wall of tossing branches behind it. She wondered if Jo by this time had come back from the river. He had not been anywhere around when Professor Hat-field and she returned from the bluff, and just a few minutes before the car had driven up, the professor had

gone again to his cottage to look for him. It occurred to
her that it could not be much more than an hour and a
half ago that he had left for his swim, though it seemed
like yesterday. He had said the beach was only a mile upstream, but perhaps in his eagerness to persuade her to go
with him he had minimized the distance. And then, as she
recalled that scene, pushed so far away by what had happened since, it struck her that, after all, he had not tried
to persuade her very hard. Doubtless she could not
measure the depths of masculine fatuity; but could even
Jo really have thought that she would go for a nudist swim
with him in the river? Perhaps again he had merely
wanted to get rid of her. For what purpose? But she had
lived through so many actual horrors to-day that she had
no longer the energy to speculate on the unknown. In a
sane world it would be fantastic to suspect Jo of such a
brutal crime; but apparently the world was not sane – at
least the world in this valley. Perhaps the only thing you
could do was to cling with desperation to your own sanity.
Meanwhile she had a task before her.

June had flung herself into the chaise-longue, and Kate
sat on the bed. As Kate told her of the afternoon she did
not once interrupt. It almost seemed as if she were too
tired to take it all in; but when Kate had finished, June
stood up quickly.

'Where's Ruby now?' she asked.

'I don't know', Kate said. 'Perhaps she's still with
Felix.'

'I don't believe she'd stay out there in this rain', June
said. 'I'm going down to her room, Kate, to see if she's
come back. I don't know what Felix has done, but she was
crazy about him. I guess I'm her best friend around here.
I guess I'm the only person she might like to see.'

It struck Kate as a pathetic commentary on the Gladstone family that the person about whom June should

show most concern was Ruby. However, the next instant she had to revise her impression, for June turned in the doorway, waited a moment for a peal of thunder to subside, and then said:

'I wish you'd go down to see Father, Kate. He doesn't say much but I know he likes you a lot. Clotilde's death will be a bad shock to him. If you'll be nice to him now, just at first, it will make it a little easier.'

'And how about you?' Kate asked.

'I might be of some help to Ruby,' June said, 'but not to Father.'

And before Kate could protest she had stepped out into the dark hall.

Glancing from her window, Kate noticed that now there was a light in Jo's cottage. The rain was falling more gently; the breeze had subsided, and she could see, scattered across the turf, a litter of torn leaves and twigs.

She walked quickly downstairs through the dusky house. She had seen, as she passed Mavis' room, that her door was still closed, and it gave her an odd feeling to think that Mavis even now knew nothing of what had happened. Kate suspected, however, that the thing she would most regret when she woke up would be having missed the thrill of the first disclosures.

The lights were on in the living-room. Mr. Gladstone was sunk in an arm-chair near the fireplace; Professor Hatfield was leaning against the mantel. Each of them had a glass in his hand.

'My dear Kate,' Mr. Gladstone said as she came in, 'I must apologize for a certain lack of cheer about the house. My dear wife, who I'm told is still sleeping off a drunk, is probably acting more sensibly than any of the rest of us. Which reminds me, let me get *you* something. You look as if you needed it.'

He rose from his chair before she could stop him. 'No,

12

no', he exclaimed. 'It's still a pleasure to get a drink for a pretty girl – but that's about all I feel up to. Would you like Scotch or bourbon?'

'I don't really know the difference', Kate said. 'I wish you wouldn't bother.' There was something very pathetic to her in Mr. Gladstone's attempt, even now, to maintain his jaunty manner.

'I think Jo has come back', she told Professor Hatfield, as Mr. Gladstone went for the whisky. 'I saw a light in his room.'

'I thought he might have', Professor Hatfield said. 'Ralph stepped out just a minute ago to see. I shall be curious to hear his adventures, if any, though I rather suspect his afternoon, from the time he left his room, will have been completely uneventful.'

He cocked his head as if he had caught in the distance the note of some rare warbler. Then he walked quietly across the room and looked out over the lawn and the drive.

'It's probably as well Jo has got home,' he exclaimed, 'because here at last are the police. They will certainly want to question everyone. I'm afraid we may even have to disturb Mavis.'

'Will the questioning be long?' Kate asked, not so much in alarm as in pure weariness.

Professor Hatfield smiled at her reassuringly.

'You and I will be the ones who have most to tell', he said. 'It's a pity Mavis can't exchange rôles with you. But I'm sure they'll be nice to you, my dear. I made the acquaintance of Inspector Waters last summer, and several others. In fact, they've done me the honour of consulting me once or twice, quite unofficially. They know I have a weakness for crime.'

*   *   *   *   *

It must have been nearly eleven when Kate stepped out on to the dark terrace. Inspector Waters and the two men with him had gone into Mr. Gladstone's study, and one by one the household had been summoned for questioning. Most of them had remained only a few minutes, but Jo and Ruby had each been kept for at least half an hour, and she herself had been almost as long. As they sat waiting in the living-room, trying to seem unconcerned, wondering who would be next, it had made her think of some lugubrious and endless game, the kind you used to have to play with children you hardly knew at birthday parties.

After dinner, which Emmy Larson had cooked and which had not been served until nine, Kate had taken two liqueur glasses of brandy, but this had had merely the effect of making her thoughts move around her in dark blurred circles. Mavis had hurried from the table in the midst of the meal and had not returned; Professor Hatfield had gone home; Jo had retired to his room, convinced, so he said, that he had caught pneumonia, and Ralph, more restless than ever, had gone for a walk. When she had stepped outside a minute ago, the only people left in the room were Mr. Gladstone, with the brandy still beside him, trying to concentrate on a chess problem, and June scowling to herself as she read *Little Women*. Kate thought there might still be policemen about the place, but she was not sure.

The air was sweet and cool after the storm. The sky was filled with stars, and she recognized Vega as she had done on her first evening. That was only three nights ago; and there was a whole month before her. Could she bear to keep on living here, in this valley, day after day, week after week? As she thought of the succession of events since Felix had knocked at her door back in Woodside, with their ghastly climax on that dark woodland path, it seemed to her that she had been groping her way through the narrowing circles of an inferno, walking down and down to an unimaginable gloom.

She heard a step on the tiles behind her, and turning she saw that Ralph had just come out of the living-room. She had never been so glad to see anyone in her life; but the next instant she felt more depressed, more lonely than ever, because she realized that of course Ralph would not be staying. There was no longer any reason why he should.

'Oh Ralph', she exclaimed. 'I'm so glad you turned up! I couldn't bear it in the house. And out here I've been sort of drowning in all kinds of black, sticky thoughts. It may be just because I'm a little drunk. I hope so. But if this is what it feels like to be drunk, I must say I can't see the attraction.'

He took her arm and led her towards the edge of the terrace. 'And am I glad to see *you*!' he exclaimed. 'You know why I went walking after dinner? Because I felt it wasn't decent to want to see you so much the very day I'd learned Clotilde was dead. But then I thought, why shouldn't I want to see you? It wasn't because of what I felt for Clotilde. I have no feeling for Clotilde any more. Not even hate. Not even pity, because she is not there any longer to be pitied. No, it was just a couple of words: I had been her "fiancé"; we had been "engaged"; and so the correct thing was to show a discreet display of bereavement, like going into light mourning. The hell with it! I guess I may be a little drunk, too. Come on, let's walk down into the garden. I've got some questions I want to ask you. First and foremost: What are you going to do now? You're certainly not going to stay here?'

'Oh yes I am', Kate said, and she was glad he had spoken, because it was so much easier to answer someone else's doubts than it was her own. 'Why shouldn't I?'

'I should think you'd seen enough of this place already.'

'I'm not staying as a vacation', she said. 'I came out

here to be with poor June. I feel now that she needs me more than ever.'

'Do you realize that there's still a murderer at large?'

'He's probably miles away by this time,' she said, 'and at any rate, he's not after *me.*'

'How do you know who he's after? Weren't you surprised when you found Felix had been killed?'

'Yes,' she said, 'I was. Please don't make me think of it now.'

'I want you to think of it', he said fiercely. 'I want to rub your nose in it, if necessary. I want you to realize that this is no place for you to stay.'

They had stepped down over the wet grass into the garden, and now he was pressing her arm almost roughly as they walked up the central path towards the sundial.

'Well, really, Ralph,' she said with a nervous artificial laugh, 'after all, that's something I'll have to decide for myself.'

'If you want to be a little fool,' he exclaimed, 'I'm going to stop you, whether you like it or not. Day before yesterday, by the tennis court, you told me I lacked detachment. Perhaps I did. It's hard to be detached about oneself. You talked about romantic self-sacrifice! Well, that particular problem was solved for me without my lifting a finger, which may have been just as well. It doesn't do much to boost my self-esteem, but I probably would have made a mess of it. The one thing that might have saved me would have been listening to you. Now you're going to listen to me. I'm not going to have you running any more risks, for all the Junes in the world. I know June much better than you do. She's quite able to look out for herself, believe me.'

His voice, in its intensity, had grown louder; though Kate felt it was perhaps the brandy she had drunk that made it seem so loud, so all-enveloping. The night pressed softly about her. She felt a longing to give way before this urgent voice, to close her eyes, to let herself be carried far from this valley to a warm safe place where she could sleep. She must struggle against it.

'If only you would stay here, too, Ralph', she said; and she knew that this was a feeble compromise, that she must begin again.

But before she had the chance, Ralph was speaking.

'Do you think anything will drag me away,' he exclaimed, 'as long as you are here? But damn it, I keep forgetting I'm not a free man! The Navy may be calling me at any time. That settles it! If you don't tell Mr. Gladstone tomorrow morning that you're leaving, then *I* will.'

'Of course I can't bear it here', Kate said, and in spite of her efforts she could not keep her voice steady. 'You must know that, Ralph. But if I ran away like that and then anything happened to June, I'd feel horribly about it – just horribly —'

Then before she could stop herself she was sobbing violently; and Ralph had taken her in his arms and was kissing, just as violently, her wet cheeks.

'Kate,' he said, when at last he could catch his breath, 'Kate, dearest, I can't bear to see you unhappy. And this may be the worst of all, but I can't help it! I'll have had this anyway!' And once more she felt his lips on hers, on her cheeks, her eyelids.

She did not know how long it was before he was speaking to her again: 'Kate, can't you stop crying? Kate, say something! Do you find this utterly repulsive?'

'No', she said through her sobs. 'No, Ralph, of course I don't.'

'Then you do love me, Kate?'

'I don't know', she said, and as she talked her tears kept rolling into her mouth. 'I don't know, Ralph, I really don't know.'

But she knew at least that in all the times young men had asked her that question, this was the first time she had not been quite sure that she was *not* in love.

Then, to her amazement, Ralph sprang away from her and plunged into the pitch blackness between the poplars. She could hear him racing among the trees towards the tennis court; then he stopped; for a moment there was complete silence, and presently he was returning to her again.

'What was it, Ralph?' she asked, and although she did not feel especially afraid, her body had begun to tremble.

'There was someone among the trees', he said. 'Some-one spying on us, or perhaps he was hiding there for some other reason. If there had only been a moon, I might have caught him.'

'Could it be anyone from the police?' she asked.

'Why should the police bother to run away? No, this fellow didn't act like a policeman.'

'Ralph,' she exclaimed, 'I bet it's the same person that was listening to Professor Hatfield and me in the summer-house. You remember, I asked if it was you.'

For a minute Ralph did not answer, and she wondered what he was thinking. Then he said: 'Kate, as a matter of fact, it couldn't be the same man, because it *was* I that was listening outside the summerhouse. Not exactly listen-ing, but just hanging around in the neighbourhood.'

'But you told me you weren't', she said.

'I know I did. I was lying.'

'But why, Ralph? Why did you do it?'

He took her hand and held it tight. 'Because, as I told you when you caught me behind the poplar, I was going to keep an eye on you, and when you spoke of the summer-house, I saw that you really seemed worried. I thought the more scared you were, the more careful you would be; so I decided I'd let you keep on thinking it was some mysterious stranger. I must say, it didn't do much good. It may seem perfectly outrageous, but I won't apologize. I'd do the same thing again.'

He sounded so belligerent that it made her feel almost gay. 'Ralph,' she said, 'if you can lie like that, how can I ever feel safe with you? I remember especially your eyes. They were staring straight into mine.'

'Ah,' he said, 'my eyes *weren't* lying. They were expressing just what I felt. But now that I've told you the truth, Kate, you must promise me that you'll be on your guard every minute of the time until you get out of this valley. We'll have a talk with Mr. Gladstone tomorrow. Until then, do I have your word?'

'I already promised you,' she said, 'night before last. And I don't break my promises.'

Chapter Sixteen

K ATE sighed and turned over on her pillow, as the persistent voice continued, trying to break into her dreams. Sleep could change it momentarily into the rustling of leaves in a black wood, into the nipping of a small dog who was really Bobbie although her coat was mangy and red, but the voice kept on reasserting itself as a thing that could not be escaped.

With a start she realized that the voice was June's; that she was speaking urgently, softly, outside the bedroom door. Kate opened her eyes. It was broad daylight, but it must be very early.

'Katey – Katey, are you awake? You must wake up. It's very important. Open the door, Katey.'

Kate sprang from bed and let June in. She was surprised to see that she was already dressed in a sweater and skirt.

'What is it?' she asked. 'Is anything the matter?'

'Ralph says he knows who the murderers are', June said, speaking almost in a whisper. 'We're in great danger, he says. Put on some clothes, Kate, but don't make any noise. He says we must get out of here before anyone wakes up. He's going to take us to Professor Hatfield's.'

Kate blinked and tried to order her thoughts. 'Ralph!' she exclaimed. 'But where did you see him, June? Isn't it awfully early?'

'It's not six o'clock. That's the point. We must get out before anyone knows we've gone.'

'But where did you see Ralph?' Kate repeated. 'I don't understand.'

'I've been up for half an hour', June said. 'I woke up

before dawn. I couldn't get to sleep and I just couldn't lie in bed any longer. I went downstairs and took Bobbie for a walk, and when I came back I ran into Ralph on the terrace. I think he'd been up all night. Most of the time he'd been keeping watch under your window, but he'd been prowling around too. He's discovered something. I don't know how. He'll tell us on our way to the professor's, but he said I was to come for you at once. If I hadn't turned up just then, he was coming up himself to wake us.'

Kate had slipped out of her nightgown and was putting on an old woollen dress. 'But who are the people?' she asked. 'Didn't Ralph say who they were?'

'He just said I wouldn't believe him, but I know he'll tell you. He said you must remember your promise. I asked what that was and he said you'd know. But hurry, Katey! He said we must hurry, that everything depended on it.'

Kate stuck her bare feet into her walking shoes. It was as if her dream were continuing, a desperate flurried dream whose setting was the pure still light of this early morning.

'Where is Ralph now?' she asked. 'Where are we to meet him?'

'He's going to be waiting in the garden, or if he thinks it's safer he may go on to the summerhouse. Are you ready? Be awfully careful until we get outside.'

Kate closed the door softly and followed June along the hall and down the stairs. The living-room had never looked so large and clean. The sunlight streaming in the windows was as clear as the light over the yellow sand at Matunuck when you went in swimming before breakfast.

June opened the front door without a sound, and they ran along close to the house, through the drenched grass, just the way Kate had seen Felix walking through that white moonlit fog. It was easy now to move silently, be-

cause the singing of the birds was so loud that it seemed
to ripple upward through the whole valley and break in a
shower of spray along the rim of the hills.

They avoided the terrace and entered the garden
through some bushes at the side. Kate looked around her
but could see no sign of Ralph.

June seized her hand. 'Somebody else must be up', she
said. 'Ralph must have seen someone. That means he'll be
in the summerhouse. He's going to take us over the bluff
by another trail. It starts from those woods. He thought
it might be safer.'

June was pulling her now swiftly through the garden,
and in a moment they had gone through the arch, where
Kate had met Professor Hatfield; and then Kate was
following June along the dark little path.

'I feel safer now', June said. 'We can't be seen from
any of the windows.'

They hurried along in silence for several minutes; and
it was not until Kate caught a glimpse of the summerhouse
around the last curve that June spoke again.

'I bet Ralph will be glad to see you', she said. 'He's
crazy about you, isn't he?'

'I don't know', Kate said. 'I think he likes me.'

'You know damn well he likes you', June said, and her
voice sounded so much like her father's that it was
startling. 'He's in love with you.'

'Perhaps he is', Kate admitted. 'I haven't given it much
thought.'

'That's good,' June said with a throaty chuckle, 'because, Katey, you can take it from me, he won't be marrying you.'

'I'd like to know why not!' Kate exclaimed. 'Why
shouldn't he marry me?'

'You wouldn't marry him unless you were in love with
him, would you?'

'Well, suppose I am?' Kate said. 'But honestly, June, I don't think it's any concern of yours just at present.'

'Oh, I don't know', June said. 'I caught him hugging you last night in the garden. He wasn't much of a watch-dog, because I sneaked right back after he chased me off, and he never knew. I guess he must have been thinking of something else. I wonder what it was! And how about the other night, when you were bringing him back to your room? Too bad I was there to meet you, wasn't it? Too bad I didn't get out. I bet you were sore as hell when I stayed. I don't believe Father would think you'd be a good influence.'

'June!' Kate exclaimed. 'What on earth has got into you? What's the matter? Are you crazy?'

For a moment, in the shock of her surprise, she could not be angry; she could not even be scared. She simply could not believe that this coarse sneering voice was June's.

'Hush!' June exclaimed. 'You don't want him to hear us talking about him.'

They had reached the door of the summerhouse, and now June turned and seized Kate's arm. 'You go in first', she said. 'You're the one he really wants to see.' And she gave Kate such a violent push that she fell on to the floor inside.

For an instant Kate was stunned. Then her first thought was Ralph.

'Ralph', she called. 'Ralph, help! Where are you?'

June, who was standing on the threshold, had turned her back towards Kate. 'Look behind the door', she said. 'You may see something you don't expect.'

With a sharp pang of terror, Kate picked herself up and peered through the shadow on to the mildewed boards which the open door had concealed. There was nothing there.

'What did you think you'd find?' June asked. 'Ralph's

body. Why should anyone want to kill Ralph? I'd hate to
see that, because now that I'm in line to inherit Clotilde's
money, he'll be marrying *me* one of these days.'

'He won't! He won't!' Kate almost screamed, as if the
sound of her voice might wake her up. 'Let me out of
here, June! Let me out of here at once!'

June turned in the doorway to face her.

'You don't think he'd marry a big ugly girl like me, do
you?' she asked. 'You make me laugh. Men like women
but they like money even better, and when they have
plenty of money they can get all the women they want.
Just look what Father used to get, the dirty old ape!'

'Ralph loves me', Kate said frantically. 'He won't marry
anyone else, so you might as well let me go!'

'That's just it', June said with the same rough chuckle
that Kate had noticed as they had come along the path.
'Perhaps he wouldn't while you were still alive. That's
your hard luck.'

She took a step forward into the summerhouse, and Kate
cowered away from her against the wall. While June had
stood in the doorway, she had kept her hands clasped behind her; but now her arms reached forward, with their
elbows raised as high as her shoulders, so that for an
instant, as she moved nearer through the green twilight,
she reminded Kate of some gigantic crustacean deep under
the sea. And then Kate would have screamed if she could
have moved her lips or her throat, because even through
this dusk she could see that June's hands were covered by
black woollen gloves.

Chapter Seventeen

KATE looked up from her copy of *Vogue*, as Mrs. Fulton, the pretty Nurses' Aide with the long eyes, opened the door of her room.

'Professor Hatfield's here', she said. 'Do you feel up to seeing him?'

'I'd love to see him', Kate told her, and the next moment the professor, who must have been right behind her, stepped into the room, with Ralph at his heels.

'Well, I've come to keep my promise,' Professor Hatfield said, 'to tell you how it all happened, if you're sure you are comfortable enough.'

'I feel fine,' Kate said, 'except that my throat's still pretty sore.' She only hoped that Ralph wouldn't think the bulky bandage around her neck was too hideous.

Professor Hatfield smiled down at her. 'You wouldn't have much chance to talk anyhow,' he said, 'unless to put in a question now and then, so I guess that needn't delay us. But I do feel sort of guilty about this young man. He insisted on coming. Do you want me to kick him out?'

'He can stay if he behaves', Kate said, and as she met Ralph's eyes, she had the same sensation that had come over her when he recognized her on the terrace at Valley Farms; the feeling that she had entered a beloved and special region, which she had always known and where she would be always safe; but now that feeling was so intense, so unimaginably happy, that her own eyes filled with tears.

'Did you notice that Nurses' Aide?' Professor Hatfield asked tactfully. 'Daphne Fulton?'

'Yes', Kate said. 'She's my favourite of all the nurses. Her husband's in Normandy, she tells me.'

'She had quite an experience of her own around here last summer', the professor said. 'You'll have to swap stories sometime. But of course you really don't know half of yours, and the part you don't know is the most interesting part – the inside part. It's the real story; and a terrible and evil one it is.'

He paused for an instant, and Kate could almost have smiled at the gusto in his voice.

'Before I begin,' he went on, 'I'd better give you my sources, so you'll believe me. In the first place, I've talked to June several times. They let me see her whenever I want to; and I've succeeded in persuading her that it will be better for her if she admits everything. She's counting on her youth and on bad influences for her defence, and I'm sure you can trust her to put up a good one. Her father, by the way, has been most co-operative. Poor man, it was more of a shock than you might have thought him capable of receiving. He's going to testify to the way June was left to herself, to herself and Felix. He's going to describe the unhealthy and demoralizing atmosphere in which she grew up. His one relief just now, I think, is a kind of sardonic pleasure in painting himself as black as possible.'

'And what about Mavis?' Kate asked.

The professor shrugged his shoulders. 'Mavis will testify too', he said. 'I'm sure by now she's looking forward to the trial. It will be a good fat part for her – a broken-hearted Mother, a Lady with a Past, a misunderstood Artist. Oh, it will be a brilliant come-back. She'll do her best to steal the show.'

Kate smiled in spite of herself. 'But you spoke as if there were more than one source', she said.

'Yes indeed. The other one is Felix's journal. The police are very grateful to me because I found it. It was hidden in the harness room. I must confess I made a complete copy of it for my files, before I handed it over. I'll read

you a few excerpts presently. Unfortunately they will have
to be short, because most of it is not suitable reading for
mixed company, or any company except a group of hard-
boiled scientists. Felix, as one could gather from his letters,
rather fancied his literary abilities, just as Landru did –
the famous French murderer, my dear. I had a hunch that
something might turn up, so I poked around for a bit. Not
that Felix ever committed himself on paper about the kidnapping or the murder. No, it was rather an account of his
various – well, perhaps I might call them his romances,
though that is hardly *le mot juste*. June knew that he kept
a journal. That was what she was looking for in his room,
late Sunday afternoon, when she told you she was waiting
to console Ruby; but the only things she found were
Felix's black gloves.'

'But if there was nothing in the diary that involved
June —' Kate began.

'There was a great deal that involved June,' the professor said, 'and June knew there must be. But let me start at
the beginning, and then if any questions occur to you,
don't hesitate to interrupt. That's what I always tell my
classes,' he said with his dry smile, 'but they seldom take
me at my word. The whole thing began with Felix, but
what interests me most from the dramatic point of view is
the way that June, little by little, took over, without his
realizing it.

'You can open a page of his journal almost at random
and see that Felix was just the kind of man I told you
about – a kind of moral imbecile. He was clever in his
way, excessively vain and quite inordinately sensual, but
the most outstanding thing about him was his complete
lack of any moral sense. He was too lazy to be terribly
ambitious. I'm sure he derived a certain ironic pleasure
from acting successfully the trusted and respected retainer.
He had a comfortable well-paid job, and for a long time he

contented himself with playing the local Don Juan, though I suspect, from veiled allusions in his journal, and from questions I've asked about the countryside, that he was responsible for the death of more than one infant. It is somewhat of an understatement to say that his sense of paternity was not particularly strong.

'I think I mentioned to you that Clotilde, when she came home from boarding school one summer – it was three years ago – had enjoyed flirting with him. Even then Clotilde, I'm afraid, was not quite so innocent as she might have been, and she could interpret quite well the way he looked at her. I gather that he felt he was sufficiently encouraged to make some unmistakable advance, and Clotilde just laughed at him. I'll read you his own comment on the episode.'

The professor pulled from his inside pocket a roll of tissue-thin pages, and glanced through them with a serious and alert expression, as if they might be lecture notes.

'Ah yes', he said in a minute. 'Here we are : *Clotilde, my fine young friend,*' he began reading, '*some day you may come crawling to me on your knees, and then it will be my turn. You're the first woman that ever laughed at Felix Brownell, and believe me, I won't forget it!*'

The professor looked up from his paper. 'Felix didn't forget it', he said. 'He was savagely humiliated. Clotilde had been playing a more dangerous game than she knew, but – one can hardly say in this case luckily – there was a way he could recapture his self-respect without touching Clotilde, at least just then. And this is where June enters the picture.'

'But that was three years ago', Kate exclaimed. 'June was only thirteen.'

'Yes,' Professor Hatfield went on, 'it was the year after she came back from the boarding school where you had first known her, and been, she told me so herself, about the

only person who had ever shown her the slightest fondness
or affection. Of course she was not a pretty girl, but Felix
had reached an age when sometimes, for men of his sort,
extreme youth is a greater attraction even than beauty,
and June was Clotilde's sister, a member of the family. If
he could substitute June for Clotilde, his vanity would be
satisfied, at least in part, and at the same time, to speak
perhaps not quite accurately, his craving for romance. But
June and Felix were a dangerous combination. It was
when his cynical coldness and utter callousness were
mixed, as it were, in a kind of chemical compound with
June's passion and suppressed violence that crime, sooner
or later, became almost inevitable.'

He paused to clear his throat, and Kate was reminded of
that afternoon a week ago when he had sat beside her on
top of the bluff and explained about Clotilde's murder and
the letter Felix had flung from the terrace.

'I've been talking so far mostly about Felix', he continued. 'Now let's turn for a moment to June. Let's see how
everything combined to enmesh the poor child, with none
too good heredity to start with, and turn her little by little
into something that might at first glance seem monstrous.
You know the kind of household in which she was brought
up, and a few years ago it was even more confused. One
might describe it as – well, let's say a kind of high-class
bordello, to put it crudely, only here it was the hosts that
paid. I'm fond of Norman Gladstone. He has many good
traits – generosity, good nature of a sort, an exuberant love
of life – but chastity, temperance, or in fact restraint of any
kind are not among them. It takes all sorts to make a
world. June must have known, almost from her nursery
days, precisely the nature of her mother's friendships
with her succession of gentlemen guests – symmetrically
balanced, one might say, by her father's special interest in
the numerous lady visitors. Neither Mr. Gladstone nor

Mavis was the type that bothers too much about closing doors, especially if there have been many cocktails, and you may be sure there always were. And if June had not suspected, I'm sure Felix would have told her.

'June has her father's violence and recklessness, and like her mother she craves the centre of the stage. But in her youth, Mavis was very pretty; on the stage or off, she never lacked an audience; while poor June was ugly and awkward. Her mother was ashamed of her; her father ignored her – and so did everyone else, everyone except Felix, that is, and perhaps Ruby until she began to suspect how much Felix liked her. The only thing that might have been a good influence in her life was the Larson family, and June found Felix much more interesting and exciting, even before the – the association began. But not only was June ignored, and more or less made fun of (I don't think Norman ever realized how much she was hurt by the somewhat ironic manner he adopted towards her, whenever he noticed her at all) that would have been bad enough, but she had an older sister, as you know, a half-sister, who was exceptionally charming to look at, whom everyone spoiled, and who regarded June with amused contempt. To make it worse, Clotilde, as everyone knew, was an heiress, while June soon learned, very possibly from Felix, that she would have next to nothing. I don't think one could be surprised if a less emotional, a less violent child than June had allowed herself, under the circumstances, to be corrupted by such an evil genius as Felix. I've known some bad ones in my day, but even for me, as I read through his journal, I could feel at times the breath of the pit. For it was a deliberate system of corruption, a long *éducation sentimentale*, quite hellish in its thoroughness and its depravity. The fact that it was interrupted when June would leave for school only added to its piquancy during the holidays and the long summer vacations. I'll read you

a few lines, written just about a year ago, which will give
you some idea of how Felix had come to think of the rela-
tionship; and then you'll see in a minute how completely
blinded he was by his egregious vanity.

'*Felix, my lad,*' he read, '*you're a lucky dog! Talk about de-
voted slaves! Well, I guess that just goes to show the value of
education. I trained her myself, brought her up by hand, you might
say – especially made to order for Felix Brownell, Esquire, like
those girls they prepare for the harems of oriental kings.*'

'And then just one more entry – the final one. It was
written last Christmas Day, when June was home for vacation. It's only a few sentences, but it's the most revealing
in the whole journal. A new possibility had dawned,
which I'll speak of presently. After that he evidently did
not dare trust himself to paper, for fear no doubt that he
might give himself away without realizing it. Here it is:

'*Well, Felix, I think you may be in for something good. If I
say half a word, no one will ever marry her. I've set my brand on
her, and she knows it. I've got her just as surely as if she was
behind bars. My lad, you can do great things if you set your mind
to it. Nothing venture, nothing win.*'

'That entry is even more ominous than it may sound',
he said. 'June told me just the other day what his plans
were.'

He rolled up the manuscript and shoved it back into his
pocket.

'And now, my dear,' he went on briskly, 'now that you
have had a glimpse of the characters, viewed as it were
from behind the footlights, we can get on to the drama of
this spring. In a way, it was quite literally a drama; I
think June always thought of it as such; because if she
inherited her mother's craving for attention, she inherited
also her flair for acting. In fact I rather imagine that June
is a better actress than her mother ever was.'

As he paused again, Kate had a vision of Felix, standing

half-naked at the entrance to the cave. It was almost an hallucination: she could see the sweat sliding over his tight pale skin between the patches of sticky hair; she could see his head thrust forward, hyena-like, his eyes softly gloating. But it was not herself at whom he stared now, it was June, who stood there, heavy and expressionless, a lost soul unaware of its damnation. Kate shuddered and drew in her breath so sharply that it hurt her throat; but the vision was gone, and mercifully a quite trivial memory floated into her mind.

'And I thought at first that she was young and inexperienced for her age', she exclaimed. 'I remember being surprised that she was reading *Little Women*.'

'You must not forget,' Professor Hatfield said, 'that if she did have much experience that, very luckily, most girls never go through, she also lacked many of the happier and more normal experiences of childhood. June is an odd mixture of the crafty and the naïve. I rather doubt whether *Little Women* was merely a theatrical prop. I shouldn't be at all surprised if she really enjoyed it and found in it a kind of dream world that delighted and even touched her, just because it was so very far away from her own. But to go back to this spring, which marks the beginning of the tragedy in which you, my poor Kate, were involved, and which also marks the emergence of June as the leading partner in the concern. As I look back upon the whole thing, I can almost see her as a sombre young Catherine de Medici, pulling strings and balancing combinations which even Felix did not suspect until near the last, and which took no one else into account – neither Clotilde, nor Felix, nor you who were her one real friend; which considered nothing in the world but the feeding of her own sense of power, the assuaging of her own passion.

'The thing was set in motion by a letter from Clotilde in New York announcing that she was engaged and was planning to be married this summer. June insists that it was Felix who first called her attention to the fact that if Clotilde married, her mother's fortune would definitely go out of the family. I have an idea, however, that June did not need much prompting, and I suspect that the germ of the plan for Clotilde's murder originated with her; not that Felix would have shrunk from it, he didn't; but simply that he wouldn't have been so apt to imagine it. He still hated Clotilde, but his hatred, I'm sure, was nothing to the intensity of June's feeling. They devised the kidnapping plan in detail; so far they were working together, hand in glove. But then Felix made a mistake. He did not realize that June had grown up during the last three years. He had done his best to help create the depraved, lonely being she had become, but he did not suspect that like Frankenstein, he had produced a monster that would turn upon himself. Felix was not satisfied with the $50,000 ransom that would be his. His wonderful plan, which at first he mentioned to June as if it were merely a joke, was in the course of the next few years to murder Ruby, and Mavis, and Mr. Gladstone, so that the whole fortune would be in June's hands by the time she was twenty-one, and then he would marry her. What shocked June, what makes her angry now when she thinks of it, was not the wholesale cruelty of the scheme, not the fact that it involved the murder of both her parents, no; it was Felix's presumption that he, a servant, should think she would ever be his wife, and let him share her fortune. Already she had grown restive under his dominance; she had begun to resent his hold over her, and to be mortified by it. No doubt this feeling was increased by her seeing other girls of her own age and social position at the various schools to which Mr. Gladstone sent her. But she knew Felix too well to let him suspect this. And then Clotilde arrived about a month ago with Ralph.'

Professor Hatfield paused again, and gave Ralph a keen sidewise glance, like a parrot in the zoo, not quite certain whether to accept or to reject the cracker that is pushed between the bars.

'I don't know whether you realize, Ralph, that from the first moment she saw you, June fell desperately, passionately in love with you.'

As Kate glanced at Ralph she saw him blush beneath his tan until he was almost copper-coloured.

'I did notice at first,' he said, 'that she was always tagging after me. She used to brush against me sometimes, as if she was a great big dog. I never liked her; in fact she sort of repelled me. I hated seeing Kate with her. Whatever June felt for me, Professor, I don't think you could call it love.'

'Call it what you will,' he said, 'she wanted you more than she had ever wanted anything in her life; she wanted you for keeps; she wanted you as her husband. I spoke of her strange naïveté; here's an example of it. She was convinced that if Clotilde was out of the way and she became an heiress, she could persuade you to marry her. Perhaps it was not so naïve, after all: she was only judging you on the basis of her own experience of people which was not a fortunate one, although undoubtedly part of your charm was the fact that you were quite different from anybody she had ever known.

'As soon as she had made up her mind that the thing she wanted most in the world was to be your wife, she began making plans to accomplish her desire. This new scheme would coincide at first with the one she had worked out with Felix; Clotilde must be got rid of, and as quickly as possible, because June was afraid you might elope or Clotilde might make a will. It was barely possible that Clotilde had done this already, but she would have to take that chance. But once Clotilde was out of the way, her plan differed considerably from Felix's little scheme, the main difference being that Felix himself must be disposed of; because she knew she would not be safe as long as he lived. He would probably not murder her; it would not be worth his while; Felix would only kill for profit; but he would be sure to blackmail her.'

'I can see why she wouldn't want *me* around,' Kate said, 'but then why did she invite me to come, and then get her father to urge me when I refused?'

Professor Hatfield beamed at her. 'My dear,' he said, 'it's at this moment that you enter upon the stage; the good character who comes in fairly late, when the play is half over, to emphasize by contrast how very bad the rest of them are.'

'You include me in that?' Ralph asked.

'I should consider you one of the more neutral characters,' Professor Hatfield said judicially, 'but on the whole the fairly sympathetic one of a young man placed in a rather awkward position. But now to answer Kate's question: June quite definitely did want you, my dear, and that was where she made her fatal mistake, as she realized only too soon. Although she was pretty confident that a million dollars or so, for I think it amounts to that, would be enough to purchase Ralph, she wanted desperately to be as attractive in his sight as possible. She knew that she couldn't dress, that she couldn't arrange her hair, that she couldn't choose the right cosmetics. I'm sure Clotilde's sarcasm would have told her this, if she hadn't guessed it without. Like many ugly hearty-looking people, she was terribly sensitive about her appearance, and that sensitivity was increased tenfold now that she had a special reason for looking her best. She remembered how kind you had been to her at school, how beautifully you had dressed and how nice you had always looked. She felt, and I'm sure she was right, that with your help she could be made, herself, far more smart and attractive.'

'But then why did I get the warning to stay away?' Kate asked.

'Ah, but you recall that now we have two people to deal with, whose interests are opposed. Naturally June couldn't tell Felix why she wanted you to come. Naturally enough Felix could only see that you would be a nuisance, an added complication, and June had to pretend to agree with him. However, she did get the warning delayed until the last minute, and if it had scared you off, I think June would have written another pathetic letter to try to persuade you. Well, you arrived that Thursday afternoon, and for the first few hours June was delighted. She had great hopes, and also I think that her kind of friendship for you was the one glimmer of disinterested affection she had ever known in her life. She told you about the note she had received, which was of course a red herring, partly to divert suspicion from her but most of all to suggest that sinister strangers were prowling in the neighbourhood, strangers who would naturally be blamed for the kidnapping. Ruby's letter was genuine. Felix knew her jealousy and wanted to scare her if he could, so that she wouldn't be in the way when the time came to dispose of Clotilde. But it must have been a severe shock to June when she found out that you and Ralph were old friends, and I think she began to suspect that very first evening that Ralph was falling in love with you.'

'I remember that she did urge me to leave', Kate exclaimed. 'It was while the men were searching the woods, right after Felix flung the letter into the garden. She was quite passionate about it, but I thought it was all for my sake.'

'Hardly that', Professor Hatfield said. 'If she had been surer of how you felt, she might have been ever more insistent. Though she probably wouldn't dare to say too much; it might have looked suspicious. And of course she hoped that you might not respond to Ralph's charms. Apparently she soon lost that hope, though I'm in no position to say why. Perhaps because she couldn't conceive that anyone could resist him, if he tried to make himself agreeable. The actual murder of Clotilde, that Thursday night, occurred as I described it to you. June swears that she did not herself help Felix, and I don't think she did. She would avoid that risk if she possibly could. We know how Bobbie upset the smooth working of the plan.

'This of course disturbed Felix, who was already beginning to suspect from June's manner that something was wrong. He had seen the way she looked at Ralph and doubtless noticed her growing jealousy of you. She told me that she found you talking with Ralph by the tennis court, Friday afternoon, in what seemed to her a rather intimate manner, and to use her own expression, it just about burned her up.'

'Just a little while after that,' Kate interrupted, 'when I was fixing her for dinner, she told me that she had overheard Mavis talking scandal about Ralph and me. I suppose she was just trying to keep us apart.'

'No doubt of it', Professor Hatfield said. 'Mavis, as you may suspect, is not averse to talking scandal, but here is one instance when I'm sure she was maligned. It was that Friday night – the night after the murder – that Felix came up to June's room. That was nothing new, except that now you were sleeping in the room next to it. He threatened to let Ralph know of their relations, if she had any idea of backing out, or turning against himself. June was furious, and it was their quarrelling voices that wakened you, Kate, that and Felix when he left to go downstairs. I'd sort of wondered at first how Felix could have roused you if he had come directly from the kitchen, and also why he had used the front door. I think it was his coming to her room that night, when June definitely did not want him to, and daring to threaten her, that determined her to get rid of him as soon as she possibly could. It had both frightened her and made her very angry; and June's anger is no laughing matter.

'The whole arrangement for leaving the ransom was excellent, I thought. I don't know which of them deserves the greater share of credit for it. Of course the notes had been put in their hiding-places several days before, and June never took the actual ransom money with her. She slipped it to Felix and got from him in exchange a dummy package which she put into her knapsack. That must have been Saturday, after lunch, just before you started out together to deliver the money.'

'But she couldn't have given it to Felix', Kate said. 'I was with her when Mr. Gladstone put it into her hands, and she never left me for a moment afterward until we left the package in the ruined house.'

'Think carefully', Professor Hatfield said. 'She must have.'

And suddenly Kate remembered. 'Of course!' she exclaimed. 'Just as we were about to start, June said it would be nice to take some Coca-Cola along and ran back into the kitchen to get it out of the icebox. She was only gone a couple of minutes.'

'That would be quite enough,' Professor Hatfield said, 'and June was justly proud of the arrangement about leaving the package, so neither Felix nor she would have to go after it; because of course if it were found there later, it would arouse suspicions. When she went into the closet, she thrust it through a hole in the plaster beneath the shelf, so that it fell down into the wall.'

'But tell me one thing', Kate said. 'If June was so eager to get me out of the way, why didn't she choose to do it that afternoon? She'd have had plenty of chances.'

'There were several reasons', Professor Hatfield explained. 'In the first place, it's possible that she hadn't quite made up her mind. Perhaps something happened afterward that precipitated matters.' He glanced from Ralph to Kate and then continued in his confidential voice: 'But the main reason is that she didn't dare to while Felix was still alive. If Felix already suspected how things stood, she knew that this would be a give-away. If she wanted Ralph enough to kill you out of jealousy, Felix would know that he couldn't count on her for himself. And also it would take some skill to explain what had happened, to prevent suspicion falling on her. Perhaps though, if she could have been sure to make it seem an accident, so sure that even Felix would be duped – On the whole, I'm rather glad that I was in the offing. Of course, as you know, I'd been keeping my eye on you. When I saw you, on the top of the bluff from my shack, that same Saturday afternoon, I thought I'd tag along. I was a little nervous when you sat for such a time on the beach, at the top of the island, because from where I was hidden I couldn't see you.'

Suddenly Kate felt once more that kind of shiver she had known so well a week ago.

'When we were sitting there on the sand bar,' she said, 'June suggested going in swimming. Do you suppose she thought then that she might drown me?'

'It's quite possible', Professor Hatfield said. 'She certainly may have toyed with the idea. Of course when you left the island it was clear that you knew someone was tracking you, and June could do nothing then even if she had wanted to. I think she was as much startled as you were. The thing that must have scared her most was that it might be Felix and that he was going to strike in some way himself before she could strike first. But she overestimated him, or rather perhaps he underestimated her. She knew that he was going to bury Clotilde's body the

next day. You recall how on Sunday afternoon, with Ralph
and her father sent off to rescue Clotilde, she said she was
going to take a nap. But her plan from the first was to slip
away to the path if she could. That low ledge above the
path, with the junipers overhanging, makes a perfect ambush. She told me she had hidden the axe there several
evenings before. It was simple enough for a husky girl
like her to split open Felix's skull from that point of
vantage. She had seen you go up the path some time ago.
She suspected you were looking for her, but she knew you
were out of the way; so she ran along the base of the bluff,
keeping just out of sight of the house, in the woods, and
joined the road after she got beyond the barns. Then she
simply sat down and waited for the car with Ralph and
her father. I guess that about clears everything up, doesn't
it?'

Kate thought for a minute: it was hard to believe that
Professor Hatfield was talking of a place where she had
actually lived herself; it was rather a region she had read
of long ago, in some dark fairy tale.

'There's one thing more', she said. 'Suppose you hadn't
turned up so early Monday morning, suppose June had
succeeded when she lured me to the summerhouse,
wouldn't it have looked suspicious to find my body there?'

Professor Hatfield smiled. 'After your midnight trip to
the front door,' he said, 'I think it would have seemed
quite natural. Doubtless June thought of that when she
made her plans. She would have come quietly back to the
house, gone to bed again, and you would not have been
missed for several hours. When you were discovered,
people would have assumed that this time you had gone
even further, actually out into the night, and that the unknown man who had killed Felix had afterward killed
you.'

'But how did you suspect that June was that unknown

person? You're so wise, I just take it for granted, but you must have had some reasons.'

'I had two very good reasons,' he said, 'but it wasn't very wise of me not to think of them sooner. They only occurred to me about three o'clock Sunday night – or rather Monday morning – and then I realized how dangerous your position might be. If there had been no outside accomplice, there obviously had been no mysterious blankets and whisky bottles tucked away in a cave in the cliff; and yet June had described them to you to explain the reasons for the warning note she had received. The fact that she lied to you about it was pretty good proof she knew the note was a fake. And then I remembered that it wasn't Mavis but June who first called attention to the figure moving in the dark, on Thursday evening, just before Felix threw the letter into the garden. June mentioned it to you, and Mavis overheard. June had taken care that she should. She knew her mother wouldn't slip any chance for a bit of drama. Of course I couldn't be completely certain, but I thought I'd better not risk going back to sleep. It's just as well I didn't.'

Ralph rose from his chair, came over to the bedside, and gazed down at her.

'Kate,' he said, 'you told me out at the farm that I loved to rescue people, and yet you see I didn't even have the luck to rescue you. I'd been prowling around all night, and when you were in the summerhouse with June, I was keeping an eye on Jo's cottage. That's why I didn't reach you until after the professor. I seemed to be doomed to stand on the sidelines and just watch things happen.'

Though his tone was serious, his effort to make it sound bitter was not too successful. Kate felt that the look with which she greeted him must have given her away, but that Ralph, characteristically, to spare her embarrassment, was pretending he had not understood.

'Perhaps before long,' she said quickly, 'when you're on your ship, you may be rescuing soldiers and marines, and that's much more important.'

Suddenly he smiled. 'Who's being romantic now?' was all he said; but his glance was so direct, so ardent, so tender and so amused that Kate blushed to her eyes; and for the first time in her life she did not mind it.

Professor Hatfield rose also. 'And now, my dear Kate,' he said, 'I must run along. You can flatter yourself that you have been involved in an exceptionally lurid case. As it stands, it should rank with the affair of Constance Kent, or of Madeleine Smith. Constance was a sixteen-year-old English girl of excellent family, who beheaded, or just about, her small half-brother and threw his body into a cesspool. Madeleine was also most respectable, and very attractive, they say. She was accused of giving her lover arsenic, not because he would not marry her, but because he insisted on doing it. But I can't help thinking what this case of ours might have grown into, if it had been allowed to develop. It was really your fault, Ralph, for throwing a wrench into the gears. You say you just stand on the side-lines and watch things happen. I should say that in this case, at least, you were the centre pin around which everything revolved. If you hadn't been engaged to Clotilde and come to the farm, June wouldn't have fallen in love with you. In that case she might have been finally induced to agree with Felix's plans; and then not only Clotilde but all the rest of her family would have died, very naturally, I'm sure, in various ingenious ways. On the other hand, Felix might have been spared – but I don't think you need feel too badly about that. Felix and June were a wonderful team to create a really magnificent example of mass murder, though I suspect that, sooner or later, one of them would have finished off the other. Still, they could have accomplished a lot first.'

He shook his head and his tone was almost wistful.

'I've learned one thing at any rate', Kate said. 'If I ever get another anonymous letter, I'll do exactly what it tells me to. Felix and June gave me fair warning. They said that if I went to the farm, I'd be sorry.'

'I hate to sound unsympathetic,' Ralph said, 'but frankly, all things considered, I'm damn glad you did.'

The professor, with his hand on the door, turned towards him. 'You're not coming with me?' he asked.

'No', Ralph said. 'I'm staying.'

THE END

www.ingramcontent.com/pod-product-compliance
Lightning Source LLC
Chambersburg PA
CBHW030320180626
46810CB00003B/1164